D0486253

HELP!
I'M TRAPPED IN
MY LUNCH LADY'S BODY

HELP!
I'M TRAPPED IN
MY LUNCH LADY'S BODY

TODD STRASSER

AN
APPLE
PAPERBACK

SCHOLASTIC INC.

New York   Toronto   London   Auckland   Sydney

Mexico City   New Delhi   Hong Kong

ISBN 0-590-97805-5

12 11 10 9 8 7 6 5   0 1 2 3 4/0

Printed in the U.S.A.   40

First Scholastic printing, March 1999

HELP!

I'M TRAPPED IN
MY LUNCH LADY'S BODY

PART ONE
THE ATTACK OF
VEND-A-LUNCH

1

"**W**e can do it. I *know* we can," insisted my friend Andy Kent. He and I were waiting on the lunch line in the school kitchen. Julia Sax, one of the grade brains, was right behind us.

"The question is *why* would you *want* to do it?" said Julia.

"Because it's there," Andy said.

"What's there?" I asked.

"I'll explain later," Andy said. We slid our trays along the silver rail past the glass cases filled with food. Barry Dunn stood in line ahead of us. Barry had short blond hair and a couple of earrings. He was big and loved to push kids around.

"Hey, lunch lady," Barry said, "whatcha got today?"

"Hamburgers and French fries," answered a heavy lunch lady with a red face and a hair net.

"Okay, gimme one," Barry said.

The lunch lady handed Barry a plate. Barry frowned. "I only got ten fries."

"That's how many you're supposed to get," replied the lunch lady.

"This one shouldn't count." Barry held up a small fry. "It's a runt."

"Oh, all right, give it back." The lunch lady reached across the counter with a gloved hand and took the fry. When she wasn't looking, Barry opened his hamburger bun and slid the burger under a napkin on his tray.

"Is this one better?" The lunch lady handed Barry a full-size fry.

"Yeah, but I didn't get a burger." Barry showed her the empty bun.

"That's strange." The lunch lady frowned, then took the bun back and gave Barry another hamburger. Andy and I shared a look. Barry had tricked her into giving him a free burger, but if we told on him, he'd kill us.

Amanda Gluck was next in line. Amanda wore thick glasses and was a teacher's pet. "Peanut butter and jelly, please."

The heavy lunch lady gave her a sandwich, but Amanda gave it back.

"Too much jelly," she said.

The lunch lady gave her another one. Amanda gave it back. "Too much peanut butter."

The lunch lady tried to give her a third one. Amanda didn't even bother taking it.

"The bread's too mushy," she complained.

"For Pete's sake, Amanda," Andy grumbled. "Just take one already. You're holding up the line."

"I'd like to see *you* eat a mushy peanut butter and jelly sandwich," Amanda replied in a huff.

"I wouldn't," Andy said. "If I wanted a peanut butter and jelly sandwich I'd bring it from home. What's the point of buying one here?"

"Because I like the ones they have here," Amanda said.

"Then why do you keep giving them back?" I asked.

Amanda stuck her nose up in the air. "Because I want the *perfect* peanut butter and jelly sandwich."

Amanda finally gave up and took a hamburger instead. Andy and I got our lunches and slid our trays down the rail to the cashier. Barry was paying for his lunch. He reached into his pocket and gave the cashier a dollar bill that was crumpled into a ball.

The cashier was skinny with lots of makeup that made her cheeks red and her eyes dark. Her black hair was teased up all around her head like a lion's mane.

"Why can't you kids carry your money in wallets like normal people?" she complained as she unfolded the bill.

"Gee, I never thought of that," Barry answered, acting dumb.

"*Ahhhh!*" the cashier screamed and jumped off her stool. Barry's dollar fell to the floor. A small toad crawled out and started to hop away. Kids started screaming and pointing.

Meanwhile, Barry calmly picked up his dollar and his tray and walked away.

2

After the commotion died down, Andy and I sat at a lunch table.

"Can you believe it?" I muttered. "Barry not only got a free extra burger, but he got away without paying!"

"Those lunch ladies really take a lot of abuse," Andy replied as he slid the wrapper off his straw and stuck the straw into a carton of chocolate milk.

"They deserve it," said our friend Josh Hopka as he joined us from the other side of the cafetorium. "It's a dumb job. Anyone who wants to be a lunch lady deserves the grief she gets."

Instead of going through the lunch line in the school kitchen, Josh had gotten his lunch from a row of new vending machines that stood along the side wall of the cafetorium.

"I can't believe you guys are still munching that mealy mystery meat the lunch ladies serve when you could be savoring a superb Vend-A-

5

Burger," Josh said. On his tray was a white Styrofoam container holding a Vend-A-Burger, Vend-A-Fries, and a chocolate Vend-A-Pudding. A tall white Styrofoam cup held a Vend-A-Shake.

"Isn't the vote coming up soon?" I asked.

"Tomorrow," said Josh as he dipped his plastic spoon into his chocolate Vend-A-Pudding. "And it looks like Vend-A-Lunch is going to win."

Andy and I scoped out the cafetorium. Josh was right. A lot more kids were chowing down with Vend-A-Lunches than school kitchen lunches. The Vend-A-Lunch Corporation had put its vending machines in our cafetorium on a trial basis. We were going to vote on whether to switch to the Vend-A-Lunches completely or get rid of the vending machines and stick with the old school lunches.

Coming toward us was a short lunch lady with muscular arms, a tattoo, and just the slightest hint of a mustache. Her short brown hair was tucked under a hair net.

"Uh-oh, look out!" I whispered. "Here comes the Lunch Lady from Hades."

"Sit up straight, Josh," she ordered.

"Sorry, Ms. Lunch Lady." Josh sat up straight.

"Is that the way they teach you to eat at home?" snorted the lunch lady.

"I'm sorry?" Josh said.

"Eating your dessert first," she said. "Is that how you do it at home?"

"No, but — "

"You should eat your lunch first and *then* your dessert," barked the Lunch Lady from Hades.

"Sorry, Ms. Lunch Lady," Josh said again.

"And *you*!" The lunch lady glared at Andy, then pointed at the floor. "Is that the wrapper from your straw?"

Andy looked down at the floor and nodded.

"Then you'll pick it up and four other pieces of garbage as well," she ordered. "That's the rule around here. Drop one, pick up five. Now do it!"

Andy quickly got out of his seat, found five pieces of garbage, and threw them in a garbage can. Then he jogged back to the table.

The Lunch Lady from Hades crossed her arms and glowered at him. "Did I just see you run?"

"It was more like a fast walk," Andy tried to explain.

"Go back and walk five times," she ordered.

"Aw, come on," Andy groaned.

"You heard me, now do it!" the lunch lady barked.

We watched as Andy walked back and forth from the table to the garbage can five times.

"That's more like it." The lunch lady with the faint mustache nodded and marched away.

"What's with her?" Josh grumbled.

"You'd be ticked off, too, if a bunch of kids were about to vote on whether you got to keep your job," Andy said.

Just then a small group of kids carrying hand-written signs came into the cafetorium. They were chanting:

> *"Two, four, six, eight,*
> *Who do we appreciate?*
> *Lunch ladies! Lunch ladies!*
> *Yay! Lunch ladies!"*

The signs said SAVE THE LUNCH LADIES, VOTE YES FOR HUMANS, STYROFOAM GO HOME!, and VEND-A-LUNCH MEANS THE END-A-LUNCH.

And the person carrying the biggest sign and chanting the loudest was my sister, Jessica.

3

"Shouldn't Jessica be over at the high school?" Josh asked.

"You'd think so," I said.

Jessica saw me and led the chanting group to our table.

"Join us, Jake," she said. "Get your friends. We need help to fight the Vend-A-Lunch Corporation."

"Why?" asked Josh as he bit into his Vend-A-Burger.

My sister narrowed her eyes angrily when she saw what he was eating. "Aren't you worried about the environment and the lunch ladies?"

"What about them?" Josh replied with a shrug.

"Styrofoam packaging ruins the environment," my sister said. "And the lunch ladies will lose their jobs if you vote in favor of Vend-A-Lunch."

Josh pointed at the Save-the-Lunch-Ladies sign. "Considering how fat some of those lunch ladies are, don't you mean Save the Whales?"

"That's lunch lady abuse!" cried Jessica's best friend, Cathy. The rest of the protesters glared angrily at Josh.

"Hey, I was only joking," Josh sputtered.

"It's not funny," said my sister. "Lunch ladies are real people just like you and me. How would you like it if someone made jokes about *you*?"

"My friends do it all the time," Josh replied.

"Then I feel sorry for you," said my sister. "But not as sorry as I feel for the lunch ladies. Most of them have been working in the kitchen their whole lives. They work hard and do their jobs well. It's all they've ever wanted to be. It's the only thing they know *how* to be. And now that's going to be taken away from them."

Jessica held out the Save-the-Lunch-Ladies sign. "Are you going to help us protest or not?"

My friends and I shared a nervous look.

"Shouldn't you be over at the high school?" I asked.

"I have special permission to lead this protest," Jessica explained. "It's part of my civics project on change in government."

"This isn't government," Josh said. "It's school."

"For kids, school is the closest thing we have to government," replied Jessica.

"Honest, Jess," I said. "Why do you care so much about a bunch of lunch ladies?"

"Because they're an important part of our

lives," my sister answered. "They care about us. They nurture us and provide us with the food we need. Believe me, Jake, you'll miss them when they're gone."

I glanced over at the Lunch Lady from Hades, who was now making Howie Jamison walk back and forth across the entire cafetorium five times because she'd caught him running. It was hard to imagine missing *her*.

"You really think carrying signs and chanting will make a difference?" Andy asked.

"This is just the beginning," Jessica told him. "We've declared tomorrow Lunch Lady Appreciation Day. And we're going to keep protesting right up until the vote at the end of the day. Now, are you going to help us or not?"

My friends stared at me as if it was my job to come up with an answer.

Just then the loudspeaker in the cafetorium crackled to life: "*Jake Sherman, Josh Hopka, and Andy Kent, please come to the office immediately!*"

4

"**G**ee, Jess," I said. "We would've helped with your protest, but it looks like we have to go to the office."

My friends and I got up and left the cafetorium.

"Wow, I never thought I'd be this glad to get called down to the office," Josh said as we walked down the hall. "Listen, Jake, did anyone ever mention that your sister is a totally twerpy tree hugger?"

"Yes," I replied. "You do about once a week."

"Why does she care so much about lunch ladies?" Josh asked.

"Maybe she's right. How would you like it if you lost your job?" Andy asked him.

"Are you serious?" Josh replied. "My mother always says that going to school is my job. If that's true, I'd *love* to lose it."

"I'm serious," said Andy as we walked down the hall. "Don't you care about them at all?"

"All I care about is decent food," Josh said. "The garbage they make in the school kitchen is the worst. Vend-A-Lunches are twenty times better."

"I bet you wouldn't feel that way if your mom was a lunch lady," Andy said with a pout.

"If my mom was a lunch lady, she'd make better lunches than they do" Josh shot back. "You guys don't know this, but lunch ladies aren't even *human*."

"Get lost," Andy scoffed.

"I'm totally serious," Josh insisted. "They're clones. They all come from four or five basic lunch lady types. You've got the big fat type, the skinny type with big hair and lots of makeup, the tough type with a tattoo and short hair, and a few others."

"Josh, you're such an escapee from the geek farm," I mumbled with a smirk.

"It's true!" Josh insisted. "They're all kept in Lunch Lady Land. That's where they're taught to make the worst food possible. And every morning they're bussed to schools everywhere to make kids sick."

"And at night they go back to Lunch Lady Land?" I guessed.

"And they're put in cages," Josh added as we stopped outside the main office.

"By the way, guys," Andy said. "Does anyone know *why* Principal Blanco wants to see us?"

Josh and I shook our heads.

Andy pushed on the office door. "Guess we'll find out soon enough."

5

"Is that really you, Jake?" Principal Blanco asked. My friends and I were sitting in his office. Our principal was leaning across his desk, staring into my eyes.

"What do you mean?" I asked.

"You know exactly what I mean," Principal Blanco replied. "Are you Jake Sherman, or are you someone else in Jake Sherman's body?"

"I swear I'm Jake in Jake," I said.

Principal Blanco turned to Andy.

"I'm Andy in Andy," said Andy.

Our principal turned to Josh.

"I'm the Cat in the Hat." Josh grinned.

Principal Blanco frowned, then leaned back in his chair and crossed his arms. "As the three of you know, I recently had a very unpleasant experience. You tricked me into switching bodies with the movie star Erie Lake, and I found myself covered from head to foot with huge, hairy tarantulas. And I *hate* spiders."

"Very yucky," Andy said.

"Nasty critters," added Josh.

"Never liked them," I agreed.

Blanco narrowed his eyes and leaned forward again. "I've spent several weeks thinking about how I should punish you three for that prank, and you know what?"

My friends and I shook our heads nervously.

"I've made up my mind," said our principal.

"A month of detention?" Andy guessed.

"Scrubbing the gym shower room with a toothbrush?" guessed Josh.

"A five-thousand-word composition on why it's wrong to charge admission to the boys' room?" I asked.

"No," replied our principal. "You see, I've realized something. Those mild punishments mean nothing to you. So I'm not going to punish you at all."

"You're not?" the three of us asked in disbelief.

"No," said Principal Blanco. "Instead, I'm going to give you a warning. A *very serious warning*. The next time I catch you doing anything wrong — and I mean the slightest *anything* you can imagine — you will all be expelled from Burt Ipchupt Middle School forever."

6

My friends and I left the office and headed back to the cafetorium.

"Forever's a long time," Andy observed.

"You think Blanco's really serious?" Josh asked.

"After we got him covered from head to foot with tarantulas?" I said. "Oh, yeah."

"But what if the next thing we do wrong is really minor?" Andy asked. "Like I get caught shooting a rubber band or passing a note?"

"I think it's like the straw that broke the camel's back," I said.

Josh frowned. "What camel?"

"It doesn't matter what camel," I said. "It's just a saying. The point is, it may be something really small, but when it gets added to everything else, it's too much."

"You know, when you think about it, it couldn't have been a straw," Andy mused. "I mean, I could see it being a cinder block that broke the camel's back."

"Or a cement mixer," suggested Josh.

"Why would you put a cement mixer on a camel?" Andy asked.

"For the same reason you'd put a cinder block on a camel," Josh answered and stopped outside the cafetorium doors. "You guys going in?"

Andy and I shook our heads. "We're gonna go outside and play ball."

"I want to finish lunch," Josh said, and went in. "Catch you guys later."

Andy and I continued down the hall. Andy had a big frown on his face.

"What's wrong?" I asked.

"Josh is such a lame-a-zoid," he grumbled.

"You mean, about the cement mixer?" I asked.

"No, about the lunch ladies," Andy said. "Why can't he understand that lunch ladies are human beings just like everyone else?"

"I bet he does deep down," I said.

"I'm not so sure," Andy replied. "I think he's the kind of pseudopod who can't understand something unless it actually happens to him. Like, unless he — "

Suddenly Andy stopped and blinked as if he'd just had a brainstorm. I may not be a mind reader, but I had a feeling I knew what he was thinking.

"No way, Andy," I said. "Just forget it. I mean, just wipe it from your mind."

"But it would be perfect!" Andy begged. "If

18

Josh was in a lunch lady's body he'd *have* to understand."

"Have you gone wacko?" I asked. "Didn't you hear Principal Blanco just now? The next time we do anything wrong, we're toast."

"No, that's not what he said," Andy corrected me. "He said the next time *we get caught* doing anything wrong, we're toast."

"No way," I said. "I'm not fooling around with the DITS anymore. Besides, it's locked inside Mr. Dirksen's lab, and he still hasn't come back from his expedition to the Amazon."

The DITS, or Dirksen Intelligence Transfer System, was supposed to transfer intelligence from one person to another. But it always malfunctioned and switched their bodies instead.

"But you've got the mini-DITS," Andy said.

"Forget it," I said.

"Come on, Jake," Andy begged. "I just want to teach Josh a lesson. I can do it in one day."

I shook my head. "Look, Andy, I understand how you feel. But the answer is still no. If there's one thing I've learned from using the DITS, it's that no matter what you plan, something always goes wrong."

Andy pursed his lips in frustration. "Okay, Jake, if that's the way you want to be, fine."

7

After school that afternoon, Josh and I went to Andy's house.

"Ready, guys?" Andy asked eagerly as he walked his BMX stunt bike out of his garage.

"No, but what difference does that make?" Josh replied.

"Can't you get excited about this?" Andy asked. "I mean, have you ever heard of anyone doing it before?"

"Listen, phlegm-brain," Josh retorted, "I've never heard of *a lot* of things. I've never heard of anyone cutting a car tire into bite-size pieces and trying to eat it. I've never heard of anyone trying to stuff a surfboard up his nose. I've never — "

"Okay, okay, I get your point," Andy interrupted. "But this is different. Three kids on a BMX going backward is *doable*."

"Yeah, but what's the *point*?" Josh asked.

"The point is, Andy wants to try it," I said. "Everyone got their helmets?"

"Check," Andy said.

"Elbow pads?"

"Check," grunted Josh.

"Knee pads?"

"Check."

"Wrist guards?"

"Check," Andy said, pulling his straps tight. "Now here's the plan. I'm on the seat. Jake, you're on the back grind pegs. Josh, you're on the front pegs. Now we'll start off going forward — "

I didn't get home from Andy's house until dark. It took a lot of tries and a couple of falls before Andy finally decided that it was impossible to ride his BMX backward with Josh and me standing on the grind pegs. Thanks to the helmets and pads, no one had gotten badly hurt.

Back at home, Mom said Jessica was at Cathy's house, preparing for Lunch Lady Appreciation Day. The next morning when I came into the kitchen for breakfast, my sister was sitting at the kitchen table coloring in the letters on more protest signs. From all the worn-out markers lying around, I could tell she'd been up for hours.

"Jess, can I ask you a serious question?" I said. "Don't you ever feel a little silly about getting so involved in all these causes?"

Jessica sighed and put down her marker. "You really want to see the environment get destroyed?"

"No," I said. "I guess I was thinking more about the lunch lady part."

"Okay, Jake, I'll try to explain it. In the old days, when people needed something, they went to another person. If they needed money, they went to the bank and saw a bank teller. If they needed to call someone, they spoke to a telephone operator. If they needed help with some new gizmo they'd bought, they called the gizmo company and spoke to someone there. These days, the only things we talk to are machines."

"So?" I said.

"So people need people, Jake," she said. "We need to relate to each other. We can't let machines take over. Machines are impersonal. You can't bond with them."

"But what if a machine does a better job than a person could?" I asked.

"If you're talking about some dull, repetitive job like working on an assembly line, I can understand using machines," Jessica agreed. "But not jobs where people could be speaking to each other. I mean, don't you *hate* talking to machines?"

"Actually, I think it's pretty cool," I said.

My sister shook her head wearily. "Believe me, Jake, when the day comes that all you talk to are machines you'll miss talking to real people."

"The only thing I'm missing right now is breakfast," I said.

"Make it yourself," Jessica said.

"What?" I asked in disbelief. "But you always make breakfast for me."

For the past few months our mom had been leaving for work too early to make breakfast. So Jessica had been making it for me.

"See?" Jessica replied with a smile as if that proved her point.

"That doesn't prove anything!" I sputtered. "You're not a lunch lady. You're my sister."

Dingdong! The doorbell rang.

"You know who that is, don't you?" I asked. Josh and Andy had gotten into the habit of stopping by my house in the morning for breakfast. Josh's parents were away on a trip and Andy's mom went to work really early like my mom.

"They're going to be pretty peeved when they find out there's no breakfast," I warned Jessica.

"Tough," replied my sister.

I went to the front door and opened it. Only Josh was outside.

"Where's Andy?" I asked.

"He went to school early," Josh said, rubbing his hands together eagerly as he stepped past me and into the house. "So what's for breakfast? I hope it's Belgian waffles."

"Try protest signs," I said as we went into the kitchen.

Josh stared at the signs on the kitchen table. "What is this?"

"Our last chance to save the lunch ladies," Jessica answered.

"Forget it." Josh shook his head and turned to me. "Let's go grab breakfast at school, Jake."

"They don't serve breakfast at school," said my sister.

"Sure they do," Josh said. "The Vend-A-Lunch Corporation put in a Vend-A-Breakfast machine and a Vend-A-Snack machine. Come on, Jake, it'll be my treat."

Outside a car honked.

"That's Cathy," Jessica said. "Her mom's giving us a ride to school. You can have a ride if you promise to help us protest."

"No way," said Josh.

"You'll be sorry," my sister called as we left.

"We may be sorry," Josh called back. "But we sure won't be hungry."

8

Jessica took her ride to school while Josh and I walked. By the time we got to Burp It Up, my sister, four other high school kids, and Amanda Gluck were marching around in front holding the signs in support of the lunch ladies. A pile of unused signs lay on the ground near them. Jessica's friend Cathy was asking everyone who came to school to sign a petition, but they all ignored her.

When Jessica saw Josh and me, she waved.

"Come on, guys, pick up some signs," she called. "We really need your help."

I could see why. Kids were walking right past the protesters and going into school.

"Doesn't look like you've got much support, Jess," I said.

"It's just a dumb peer pressure thing," Jessica replied. "Kids are afraid that their friends will laugh at them if they join us."

"Or maybe they really like the Vend-A-Lunches better," Josh countered.

"The Vend-A-Lunch machines don't even have peanut butter and jelly sandwiches," Amanda said.

"Amanda," Josh said, "did anyone ever tell you that you're a slug-sniffing major multiple mutant?"

I grabbed Josh's arm and pulled him toward the school entrance. "Come on," I said. "Let's leave them alone."

We went inside and headed for the cafetorium, but as we passed the eighth-grade wing, I noticed Andy in the hall near our lockers.

"Hey, Andy!" I waved.

"Oh, hi, guys." Our friend waved back awkwardly.

"Want to get a Vend-A-Breakfast?" Josh asked.

"Uh, sounds great," Andy said. "You guys go ahead. I'll catch up with you in a second."

"You see?" Josh asked as he and I headed toward the cafetorium. "Even Andy doesn't mind eating the Vend-A-Stuff."

Inside the cafetorium, a small crowd of kids were standing around the Vend-A-Lunch machines. Barry Dunn was on his knees in front of the Vend-A-Breakfast machine. He'd stuck his arm up the food shoot.

"What's wrong?" Josh asked Alex Silver, who was watching.

"Nothing," Alex answered. "Barry's trying to see if he can get a Vend-A-Breakfast for free."

We watched as Barry felt around inside the machine.

"Feel anything?" Alex asked.

"Not yet," Barry answered.

"Hey, Barry," Josh said. "How about letting those of us who don't mind *paying* for breakfast get what we want?"

"Bug off," Barry grunted. He stood up and grabbed the sides of the Vend-A-Breakfast machine. Then he tilted it forward and started to shake it. Things started to rattle and bang inside. Barry got down on his knees and stuck his arm up the food shoot again.

"Any luck?" Alex asked.

"I think I feel something," Barry grunted.

"Know what I feel?" Josh said. "I feel my stomach grumbling. Know why? Because I haven't had breakfast."

"If you don't shut up you'll get a knuckle sandwich for breakfast," Barry warned him.

Brrriiinngggg! The first bell rang. It was time to go to homeroom.

"Great," Josh muttered unhappily. "Now I have to wait until lunch before I can eat."

9

As we left the cafetorium, I noticed Andy coming out of the door that led to the school kitchen.

"What were you doing in there?" I asked as we started to walk down the hall toward homeroom.

"Oh, uh, nothing," Andy said. "So did you guys get Vend-A-Breakfasts?"

"We couldn't," Josh answered. "That big bozo Barry hogged the machine trying to get stuff for free."

At our lockers, I noticed that Andy took a roll of duct tape and a small spool of bright red wire out of his backpack.

"Science experiment?" I asked.

"Huh?" Andy scowled.

"The wire and duct tape," I said.

"Oh, uh, yeah," Andy said. "Science experiment."

My friends and I went to homeroom and then to math class. After math class, we were supposed to go to gym. But out in the hall, Andy and Josh suddenly turned in the other direction.

"Where are you guys going?" I asked.

"Oh, uh, I just want to show Josh something," Andy answered.

"What?" I asked.

"Nothing that would interest you," Andy replied.

"Aren't you coming to gym?" I asked. "We have to practice for the decathlon."

"Oh, sure," Andy said. "We'll be there in a second." Then he hurried Josh away before I could ask any more questions.

As I went into the boys' locker room, I wondered why Andy was acting so weird. Where could he be taking Josh? And what could the big secret be?

I opened my locker and started to change into my gym clothes. Seconds were ticking away, but Andy and Josh still weren't back. If they didn't get there soon, they were going to be late.

Brrrriiinngggg! The bell rang just as I finished changing into my gym clothes. Josh and Andy still hadn't come to gym. Now they were definitely late.

And that meant something *definitely* weird was going on.

As I left the locker room and went out to the gym I began to think back to what had happened that morning.

Josh said Andy had gone to school early.

I'd seen Andy in the hall near our lockers before school began.

Then I saw him come out of the school kitchen.

He'd had that red wire and duct tape.

He'd said it was for a science experiment.

Howie Jamison was practicing foul shots before gym began. Howie was in Andy's science class.

"Hey, Howie," I said. "Are you guys doing experiments in science?"

"Naw," said Howie, "we're looking at junk through microscopes."

"You're not doing anything with wire and duct tape?" I asked.

Howie shook his head. "No way."

Andy had lied! I realized.

And that could only mean one thing!

The next thing I knew, I was running as fast as I could — out of the gym and down the hall. The mini-DITS was hidden on the top shelf of my locker, behind an old Burp It Up sweatshirt.

I got to my locker, opened it, pulled out the sweatshirt, and felt around.

The mini-DITS was gone!

10

I started to run. I had to get to the cafetorium before Andy used the mini-DITS to switch Josh with one of the —

"Hold it right there, Sherman!"

I skidded to a stop. Behind me, Principal Blanco came out of a classroom.

"How many times have I told you not to run in the halls?" my principal asked.

"But, uh, I'm supposed to be running," I stammered. "I'm in gym."

Principal Blanco frowned. "If you're in gym, what are you doing here in the hall?"

"I'm running," I said.

"But if you're in gym and you're running, why aren't you running outside?" Blanco asked.

"Because on rainy days we run inside," I answered.

"But it's not raining," said Principal Blanco.

"I know," I said. "But I'm practicing for a rainy day."

Principal Blanco frowned.

"Principal Blanco?" Down the hall, white-haired Mrs. Hub, one of the school secretaries, waved from the office.

"Yes, Mrs. Hub?" Principal Blanco answered.

"The ballot boxes for today's vote have arrived," Mrs. Hub said. "You have to sign for them."

"All right." Principal Blanco turned to me. "Continue with your run, Jake."

With a big sigh of relief, I started down the hall again.

I reached the cafetorium, but it was empty. Where were Josh and Andy? Voices were coming from the school kitchen. I dashed across the cafetorium and pushed through the kitchen doors. Inside, three lunch ladies were on the kitchen side of the glass display cases. On the lunch line side of the counter, Andy and Josh were leaning against the rail.

Andy's jaw dropped when he saw me. "Jake, what are you doing here?"

I didn't answer. I was too busy trying to figure out what he was planning. A bright red wire snaked out from the railing around the metal counter. Another strand of wire disappeared under the rail.

I ducked down and looked.

The mini-DITS was taped under the rail! Andy had wired it to the metal kitchen counter. He'd turned the entire lunch line into one huge DITS!

And at that very moment he was reaching under the railing!

"Don't!" I shouted.

"Don't what?" asked one of the lunch ladies.

But it was too late.

WHUMP!

BANG!

PART TWO
WELCOME TO
LUNCH LADY LAND

11

When I opened my eyes, I was lying on the floor of the school kitchen. Everything looked hazy, but five faces slowly came into focus. They were staring down at me. One of the faces was mine. The others belonged to Andy, Josh, the heavy lunch lady with the red face, and the skinny lunch lady with the makeup and big black hair.

And that could only mean one thing: I was in the body of the Lunch Lady from Hades!

"May?" said Josh, or whoever now had Josh's body.

"I'm May," said the person who now had my body.

"I'm June," said the person who now had Josh's body.

"I'm April," said the person who now had Andy's body.

"You have to be kidding," said the heavy lunch lady, who I suspected was really Josh.

"Kidding about what?" asked the lunch lady named April who now had Andy's body.

"Those names," said Josh in the heavy lunch lady's body.

"Aren't lunch ladies allowed to have names?" huffed the Lunch Lady from Hades who now had my body.

"I guess," replied Josh in the heavy lunch lady. "But April, May, and June?"

"It was a coincidence, okay?" snapped the lunch lady who had my body.

"But we think it's kind of sweet," added the heavy lunch lady who had Josh's body.

"Uh, excuse me," I said in the body of the Lunch Lady from Hades, "but unless I'm seriously mistaken, I think we're missing the point here."

"What's that?" asked the lunch lady in Andy's body.

I pointed at the skinny lunch lady with the makeup and big hair. "Who are you?"

"I'm Andy," she said.

"And I'm Josh," said the heavy lunch lady.

"And I'm Jake," I said in the body of the Lunch Lady from Hades.

"I don't get it," said the real Lunch Lady from Hades, who now had my body.

"We've switched bodies," said Andy in April's body.

"You mean, we're not lunch ladies anymore?" asked June, who was now in Josh's body.

"We're teenage boys!" gasped April in Andy's body.

"I always wanted to be a teenage boy!" cried May in my body. "Hey, June, give me a high five!"

May in my body and June in Josh's body shared a high five, a low five, and then bumped hips. The three lunch ladies in our bodies started to giggle.

"Hey, girls, watch this!" April in Andy's body picked up a small pizza and whipped it across the kitchen like a Frisbee.

"Check *this* out!" cried May in my body. She picked up a pudding and chucked it at the wall, where it made a big brown *splat*.

"And I always wanted to do *this*!" June in Josh's body grabbed an industrial-size can of Cool Whip and shot it into the air.

My friends and I in the lunch lady bodies watched dumbstruck as the giggling lunch ladies in our bodies hurled and shot food in every direction. Soon the kitchen walls, counters, and refrigerators were covered with dripping glop.

"Wait a minute!" cried June in Josh's body. "What are we doing in this stupid kitchen, anyway?"

"You're right!" gasped May in my body. "We never have to work in this hot, gross, smelly place again!"

Still giggling like crazy, the three lunch ladies in our bodies headed for the kitchen door.

"Wait!" I cried in the body of the Lunch Lady from Hades.

The lunch ladies in our bodies stopped.

"Don't forget, this is only temporary," I said. "You have to give back our bodies."

"Says who?" asked April in Andy's body.

"That's the way it's always been," I said.

"Yeah, we always get our bodies back," added Josh in June's body.

"It's part of the deal," said Andy in April's body.

The three lunch ladies in our bodies looked at each other.

"Did anyone here make a deal?" asked May in my body.

The other two shook their heads.

"Does anyone here want her old body back?" asked June in Josh's body.

The other two shook their heads.

April in Andy's body turned to my friends and me. "Sorry, boys, er, I mean, *girls*. But we like it this way."

The next thing we knew, the three lunch ladies ran giggling out of the kitchen — *in our bodies!*

12

Back in the kitchen, Josh in June's body, Andy in April's body, and I in May's shared a worried look.

"You know," said Josh in June's body, "it might not bother me so much if they'd just stop giggling."

"I know what you mean," agreed Andy in April's body. "It's so embarrassing. The three of them in our bodies running around school giggling. Everyone's gonna think it's us."

"Uh, guys," I said in May's body, "I think we're missing the point again."

"What point?" asked Josh in June.

"The point I'm trying to make," I said in May's body.

"You know, everyone always talks about these points," said Andy in April. "We're always making a point or missing the point or getting the point. Someone's always saying that this is

39

the point or that is the point. But really, what *is* the point?"

"I think it's an 'oint' with a 'p' before it," said Josh in June.

"Then what's an oint?" asked Andy in April.

"Simple," said Josh in June. "It's an 'int' with an 'o' before it."

"How do you know it's not an 'oin' with a 't' *after* it?" Andy in April asked.

Josh in June screwed up her face. "Give me a break, Andy. *Everybody* knows an 'oint' is an 'int' with an 'o' before it."

"But that's my whole point," said Andy in April.

"Excuse me, guys," I interrupted, "but I really think we're missing the point."

"Here we go again," Josh in June groaned.

"No, listen, seriously," I said in May's body. "I was talking about the lunch ladies in our bodies."

"Oh, right," Andy in April recalled. "That giggling stuff."

"Well, don't get me wrong," I said in May's body. "I don't like them giggling, either. But what really worries me is the idea that they don't want to give back our bodies. Which means we may be lunch ladies for the rest of our lives."

In April's body, Andy twirled a long strand of black hair around her finger in a thoughtful gesture. "Good point. Er, I mean, good *observation*."

"Then what do you suggest we do?" asked Josh in June's big, heavy body.

"I suggest we stop them," I said.

"I think you've got a point there," said Josh in June.

"Where?" asked Andy in April.

"Let's just go find them," I said with a sigh.

13

The three of us in lunch lady bodies hurried out of the kitchen and into the cafetorium. We didn't have to go far to find the lunch ladies in our bodies. They'd stopped by the Vend-A-Lunch machines.

"Now what?" I asked in May's body.

"Looks like they're trying the food," said Andy in April.

He, I mean, *she* was right. The three lunch ladies in our bodies were sitting at a table and sampling the Vend-A-Lunch selection.

"Not bad," said June in Josh's body after biting into a Vend-A-Burger. "Hey, April, how're those Vend-A-Fries?"

"Crispy, but not quite enough salt," replied April in Andy's body. "How's the shake, May?"

May, the lunch lady in my body, was slurping noisily at a Vend-A-Shake. "Nice and thick. I can barely get it through the straw."

"That's just the way I like them," said June in Josh.

"Uh, excuse me," I said. "How can you like that food?"

The three lunch ladies in our bodies scowled at me. "Why not?"

"Because of that food, you're all probably going to lose your jobs," I said in May's body.

"No, hon," replied April in Andy's body, "because of this food, *you're* going to lose *your* jobs."

"Good point," said Josh in June's body.

"Where?" asked Andy in April.

"Forget it," I said in May's body. Then I motioned to my friends to join me in a huddle so the lunch ladies in our bodies wouldn't be able to hear.

"Listen," I whispered. "We have to come up with a plan."

"Like what we'll do when we're not lunch ladies anymore?" guessed Andy in April, twisting some black hair around her finger again.

"You could open a hair salon," suggested Josh in June's body.

"I was thinking more along the lines of becoming an astronaut," mused Andy in April's body.

"The first lunch lady in space!" gasped Josh in June's body.

"Maybe the first lunch lady on the moon," mused Andy in April with a dreamy expression.

"Great, you could serve lunch to E.T.," I interrupted in May's body. "Guys, I hate to say this, but once again I think you're missing the . . . er, whole idea. If we don't do something fast, we're going to be lunch ladies for the rest of our lives."

"Good point," said Andy in April's body.

"Where?" asked Josh in June.

"Shut up!" I yelled in May's body. "Now, what are we going to do?"

"About what?" asked Josh in June.

"About the lunch ladies, dimwit!" I hissed.

"They're leaving," said Andy in April.

"What?" I spun around. The lunch ladies in our bodies had gotten up from the table and were walking out of the cafetorium.

"Come on before they get away!" I cried in May's body. Andy in April's body and I started to run, but Josh in June's body stayed behind to finish the Vend-A-Lunches the lunch ladies in our bodies had left on the table.

"You guys go ahead!" Josh in June's body called through a mouthful of food. "I just want to finish this stuff. Then I'll catch up!"

Andy in April and I in May got out to the hall. We turned a corner and skidded to a stop.

"Oh, no!" I gasped in May's body. "They're skipping!"

The three lunch ladies in Andy's, Josh's, and my bodies had locked arms and were skipping happily down the hall.

"They're making us look like total giggling,

44

skipping mega-wusses!" I gasped in May's body.

"But it is kind of cute," said Andy in April.

"You're crazy!" I cried. "Now we *really* have to stop them!"

"Stop who?" asked someone behind us.

Andy in April's body and I in May's turned. Behind us, Principal Blanco was coming out of the office.

14

"What are you lunch ladies doing in the hall?" Principal Blanco asked us. "Shouldn't you be in the kitchen warming up lunch?"

Andy in April's body and I in May's body shared a nervous look.

"That's exactly what we're doing!" Andy in April said. "We're, uh — "

"Warming up for lunch," I said in May's body.

"Right!" Andy nodded April's big head of hair. "Gotta stay in shape."

Principal Blanco frowned. "Why?"

Andy in April gave me a worried look.

"Uh . . . because serving lunch takes a lot of work," I explained in May's body.

"Then shouldn't you stay in shape by doing that work?" asked Principal Blanco. "Lunch ladies are not supposed to be in the halls. Please — "

Just then Josh in June's body lumbered around the corner, gasping for breath.

"Where did they go?" she panted.

"Where did *who* go?" Principal Blanco asked.

Josh in June's body took a breath. "The — "

"Other lunch ladies," I cut in.

"The *other* lunch ladies are running around the school, too?" Principal Blanco asked with a disbelieving scowl.

I knew I had to come up with an explanation . . . *fast!*

"Okay, Principal Blanco, I'll tell you the truth," I said in May's body. "It was supposed to be a surprise, but we lunch ladies have all entered, er — "

"The National Lunch Lady Decathlon," Andy in April blurted.

Principal Blanco, Josh in June's body, and I in May's all looked at him, I mean, *her*, like she was psycho.

"The *what*?" Principal Blanco said.

"The National Lunch Lady Decathlon," Andy in April repeated. "The top lunch ladies from all around the country gather each year to compete in such challenging events as, er — "

"Speed serving," I said in May's body.

"Heavy tray lifting," said Josh in June's body.

"Change making," said Andy in April's body.

"Table wiping."

"Roach squashing."

"Roach squashing?" Principal Blanco repeated with a frown.

"Look!" Andy in April's body pointed outside through the hallway window. The three lunch

47

ladies in our bodies were skipping along the walk away from school.

"Kent, Hopka, and Sherman," Principal Blanco muttered through clenched teeth. "Where in the world do they think they're going?"

"Shouldn't you stop them?" I asked innocently in May's body.

"Stop them?" Principal Blanco puffed out his chest. "I'll do more than that. I'll expel them forever!"

"But — " I began to say in May's body.

"And you three!" Principal Blanco jerked his head toward the cafetorium. "Back to the kitchen! If you want to practice for the Lunch Lady Decathlon, do it on your own time."

15

My friends and I in the lunch lady bodies trudged back toward the kitchen.

"I *told* you not to fool around with the mini-DITS," I grumbled unhappily to Andy in April's body. "Now we're going to get expelled."

"Not us," countered Andy in April's body. "Them."

"But we're them," I argued in May's body.

"No, we're us," said Josh in June's body.

I couldn't believe it! "You guys really want to be lunch ladies for the rest of your lives?"

"There are worse things," said Andy in April.

"Like what?" I asked in May's body.

"Armpit sniffer for a deodorant company," said Josh in June's body.

"Athlete's foot medicine tester," said Andy in April's body.

"The guy with the shovel who walks behind the elephants at the circus," said Josh in June's body.

"In the summer," added Andy in April's body.

"P.U." Josh squeezed June's nose.

"What are you guys talking about?" I gasped in May's body.

"Oh, look!" Andy in April's body pointed down the hall at the outside doors. "Our bus is here."

Parked in the bus circle outside was a school bus. Only instead of being yellow, it was pink. There were flowery black letters on the outside, but I couldn't see what they spelled.

"We can't miss it, girls!" cried Josh in June's body.

Josh in June's body and Andy in April's body grabbed my arms and began to tug me toward the doors.

"But, wait!" I cried in May's body. "We can't leave! We have to get back into our own bodies."

"Too late for that," said Andy in April's body as they tugged me in May's body through the doors and out to the bus circle. Now I could see the flowery letters on the bus more clearly. It said:

Lunch Lady Land

"*What?*" I dug May's feet into the ground. "There's no such thing as Lunch Lady Land!"

"Of course there is, silly," Josh in June said, still pulling on my arm. "That's where they keep us at night."

"Don't you want to learn to make gross food?" asked Andy in April.

"And the best part is, we get to try it first!" added Josh in June's body.

"No! No! No!" I screamed and fought, but it was no use. My friends in their lunch lady bodies were too strong. Like it or not, I was on my way to Lunch Lady Land!

PART THREE
RETURN TO REALITY

16

"**N**o! No! No!" I heard myself shouting.

"May, wake up!" Someone was shaking my shoulder.

I opened my eyes. I was lying on the school kitchen floor. Five faces were staring down at me: mine, Andy's, Josh's, the big heavy lunch lady's, and the skinny lunch lady's with the makeup and big hair.

"No!" I shouted. "You can't make me go to Lunch Lady Land!"

"I was kidding you, dummy," said the heavy lunch lady. She looked like June but sounded like Josh.

"No, you weren't!" I gasped. "I saw the pink bus!"

"What pink bus?" asked the lunch lady who looked like April but sounded like Andy.

I blinked and looked down at myself and saw tattoos on my arms. I was in May's body. "The pink bus that takes us back to Lunch Lady

Land, where they put us in cages at night."

"You're in the kitchen at Burp It Up Middle School," June informed me. Again, she sounded more like Josh than a lunch lady.

"Did you hear that?" giggled the kid who looked like Andy but didn't sound like Andy.

"Burp it up instead of Burt Ipchupt," chuckled the kid who looked like Josh but didn't sound like Josh.

"What's going on?" I asked in May's body.

"We all switched bodies," said the heavy lunch lady who looked like June but sounded like Josh. "I'm Josh."

"I'm May," said the lunch lady who now had my body and was wearing my gym clothes.

"I *know* that," I said. "We switched this morning." I pointed at the lunch ladies who now had our bodies. "You went off giggling and skipping while Principal Blanco caught us in your bodies and sent us back to the kitchen. And then the pink bus came to take us to Lunch Lady Land."

Everyone frowned at me.

"I have news for you," said Andy in April's body. "We only switched, like, three minutes ago. The rest of us woke up and figured out what happened. But you must've hit your head on something because you took a lot longer to wake up."

"Then . . . it was a dream?" I realized.

"No, hon," said April in Andy's body. "We really have switched."

54

"No, no, I *know* that," I said in May's body. "But the Lunch Lady Land part was a dream."

"I think so," said June in Josh's body.

"You don't all get picked up by a pink bus and taken to Lunch Lady Land every day after lunch?" I asked.

"I go home to my husband," said April in Andy's body.

"I go home to my mother," grumbled May in my body.

"I go home to Poopsie," sighed June in Josh's body.

"Poopsie?" I repeated.

"My kitty," explained June in Josh's body.

"You're not going to go giggling and skipping away in our bodies?" I asked, relieved.

"No way," said Josh in June's body. He, I mean, *she* glowered at Andy in April's body. "I'm going to stay right here and break Andy's skull for tricking me into switching bodies with a lunch lady."

"Wait a minute!" April in Andy gasped. "That's *my* skull."

"Breaking skulls isn't going to help anyone," sniffed June in Josh's body.

"All we have to do is switch back to our own bodies," said Andy in April. "Then everything will go back to normal."

"You're right," said April in Andy. "In a few hours I have to go home to my husband."

"And I have to go home to Poopsie," added June in Josh.

We all turned to May in my body. We expected her to say she had to go home to her mother. But May in my body crossed my arms and shook my head.

"Don't you want to get home to your mother?" I asked in her body.

"Get real," she grumbled in my body. "I never want to see that old bag again for as long as I live."

"You mean, you don't want to switch back to your real body and give me back mine?" I asked nervously.

"Uh, guys?" Andy in the big-hair lunch lady's body was crouched under the lunch-line railing. "I hate to say this, but it doesn't look like anyone is switching back to anything."

17

We heard a ripping sound as Andy in April pulled off the duct tape. A moment later he held up the mini-DITS. Or, I should say, what was *left* of the mini-DITS.

The miniature version of Mr. Dirksen's machine was blackened and charred. The plastic covering had melted, and little wisps of smoke were rising from it.

"Oh, no!" cried Josh in June's body.

"What is it?" asked April in Andy.

"The mini-DITS," I answered in May's body. "It's the machine that switched our bodies."

Andy shook April's head. "Forget it. It's toast."

"You mean, it's no good anymore?" asked June in Josh.

"Right," answered Andy in April. "It must have shorted out."

"Now I remember," I said in May's body. "After the *whump* there was a *bang*."

"Yeah," grumbled Josh in June, "because some dimwit tried to wire the *entire* food counter."

"I was only trying to teach you a lesson," sniffed Andy in April.

"What kind of lesson?" asked May in my body.

"That lunch ladies are people, too," said Andy in April.

With frowning faces, the three lunch ladies in our bodies turned on Josh in June's body.

"What did you think we were if we weren't people?" May in my body asked angrily.

Josh in June backed away nervously. "I . . . I knew you were people. I was just fooling around."

"Can't you fool around without picking on someone?" glowered April in Andy's body.

"Uh, sure," Josh in June replied. "I do it all the time. I — "

He was interrupted by the sound of a door opening out in the cafetorium. We heard footsteps and voices. A moment later the door to the school kitchen opened and in walked Jessica's friend Cathy and two guys from the high school. One was carrying a rolled-up banner. The other was lugging a ladder.

"Oh, hi, Jake," Cathy said to May in my body.

May in my body wasn't used to being called Jake. She didn't answer.

Cathy scowled. "Didn't you hear me, Jake?"

The lunch lady who had my body still didn't answer.

"Hey, Jake," I said to May in my body. "Cathy's talking to you."

May in my body blinked and turned to Cathy. "Oh, I'm sorry. What did you say?"

"I said hi," Cathy said. "And why are you wearing gym clothes?"

"Oh, uh — " May in my body began to answer. Worried she might say the wrong thing, I quickly interrupted.

"So what's that?" I pointed May's finger at the banner.

"Show them," Cathy said to the guy carrying the banner.

The high school guy unrolled the banner. In big letters it said:

SUPPORT LUNCH LADY APPRECIATION DAY

"Very nice," said April in Andy's body. The other lunch ladies in our bodies nodded in agreement.

"I'm glad you approve, boys," Cathy said to the lunch ladies in our bodies. "But I'd really like to know what the ladies think."

"It's okay," Josh in June replied with a shrug.

"Awesome," said Andy in April.

"Very good," I said in May's body.

"We were wondering if we could hang it in here," Cathy said. "Right above the counter where you serve lunch."

"Good idea," said May in my body.

Cathy frowned. "No offense or anything, Jake. But don't you think the lunch ladies should be the ones who decide?"

"I think May, er, Jake's right," I said in May's body. "This is a good place to hang it."

Cathy and the high school guys started to hang the banner. Meanwhile, the three lunch ladies in our bodies got into a huddle and started whispering.

Then April in Andy's body waved to us, and we followed the lunch ladies in our bodies out of the kitchen and into the cafetorium, where Cathy and her friends couldn't hear.

"Are you saying we're really stuck in these bodies *forever*?" April in Andy asked us.

"Maybe not forever," I answered in May's body. "But we could be stuck in them until Mr. Dirksen gets back from the Amazon."

"The science teacher?" asked June in Josh's body.

"Right," I said in May's body. "He's supposed to be back any day now, but no one really knows."

"By the time he gets back we may have lost our jobs," said May in my body.

"What about the protest they're supposed to have today?" asked June in Josh's body.

"I hate to say this," I said in May's body, "but most of the school doesn't seem to care."

"That's it!" gasped April in Andy's body.

"What's it?" asked Josh in June.

"This could be a blessing in disguise!" said April in Andy. "You see, when we were in our lunch lady bodies, no one would listen to us. If we said we wanted to save our jobs, they'd say of course you do, you're lunch ladies. But now that we're in the bodies of three teenage boys, people might really listen!"

"What should we do?" asked June in Josh's body.

"We have to organize!" April in Andy's body made a fist and raised it in the air. "We have to persuade and convince and sway. We have to make the students of this school believe that there is no substitute for a lunch lady, or for a lunch lady's lunch!"

"Good luck," grumbled Josh in June's body.

"Here, here!" cried May in my body.

"All for one and one for all!" cheered June in Josh's body.

Slap! The lunch ladies in our bodies shared a high five and started to march out of the cafetorium.

"Wait!" I yelled in May's body. "What about lunch?"

"That," answered April in Andy's body, "is *your* problem."

18

My friends and I in the lunch lady bodies went back into the school kitchen. It was almost lunchtime.

"What do we do?" Andy in April's body asked nervously.

"We have to be lunch ladies," I answered.

"How?" asked Josh in June's body, biting her lip with worry.

"Look, it's not brain surgery," I said in May's body. "You've seen lunch ladies serve lunch, right, Josh? Now you're gonna serve. Andy, you're a cashier lunch lady. You know how to count?"

"Of course I do," answered Andy in April.

"Then you know how to make change," I said.

"And what about you?" asked Josh in June's body.

"I'm a monitor lunch lady," I said.

"You know how to monitor?" asked Andy in April.

"Sit up straight!" I commanded in May's body.

"Eat your lunch before dessert! Walk in and out five times!"

Andy in April nodded her big head of black hair. "Yeah, you know how to monitor."

"Hey, guys, look at this." Josh in June's body was standing by the kitchen delivery door. As Andy in April and I in May walked toward her, Josh in June pulled a sheet off a motorcycle that was parked beside the door. The motorcycle had high fenders and nobby tires.

"Wow!" Andy in April gasped. "A Kazubi dirt bike! Way cool!"

"What's it doing here?" I asked in May's body.

"It must belong to one of the custodians," guessed Josh in June.

"Wouldn't it be cool to take it for a spin?" mused Andy in April.

"Give me a break," scoffed Josh in June. "You don't know how to drive a dirt bike."

"It can't be that different from a BMX," countered Andy in April. "Come on, let's try it."

"Hold it," I said in May's body. "We have to make lunch, remember?"

Andy in April's shoulders sagged. "Sorry, I forgot. So what's on the menu?"

"Tacos." Josh in June read from a sheet of paper taped to the wall.

"I've made those!" Andy in April cried. "They're easy! All you need is taco shells, lettuce, cheese, and meat."

We quickly spread out through the kitchen.

"I found the taco shells!" called Josh in June from a pantry.

"I found the cheese and lettuce," Andy in April called from the big steel refrigerator. "And it's already shredded."

In the meantime I pulled open the heavy wooden door of the school freezer. Inside were big white cardboard boxes the size of cinder blocks.

"Did you find the meat, Jake?" Josh in June asked.

"I'm not sure," I called back in May's body.

Andy in April and Josh in June came over as I pulled out one of the cardboard boxes and put it on the counter. The box was really heavy and covered with slippery white frost.

"You think this is it?" Josh in June asked.

"Look!" Andy in April started to scrape off some of the frost. "There's a label under here." She kept scraping until we could read the label:

REFREEZABLE MEALY MYSTERY MEAT

Good for hamburgers, sloppy Joes, tacos. Warning: For students only. Do not serve to teachers with discerning tastes or adults with weak stomachs. Best If Used Before Year 2599.

"See!" Josh in June said. "I *told* you!"

"You'd think they'd come up with a better name," I said in May's body.

"Makes you think seriously about becoming a vegetarian, doesn't it?" asked Andy in April.

"Not really," I said in May's body.

"Makes me think about using more catsup," added Josh in June as she began to tear open the box.

"You're not going to feed this stuff to our classmates, are you?" Andy in April asked.

"Are you ready to tell four hundred starving kids that you didn't want to make them lunch?" I asked in May's body.

Andy in April twirled some black hair around her finger. "You're right. We better hurry!"

By now we'd torn the box away. The frozen gray block of refreezable mealy mystery meat lay on the counter.

"We have to break it up." Andy in April jabbed the block with a fork.

Nothing happened.

She jammed the fork down harder.

The fork bent.

"Back off." In May's body I picked up a big meat cleaver and swung it down like an ax.

Crack! The cleaver broke off its wooden handle.

"This stuff is indestructible!" I said in awe.

"I know what'll do it." Josh in June hurried out of the kitchen. A moment later she came back with a rusty pickax. Small chunks of dirt were stuck on it.

"But it's all dirty and rusty," Andy in April said as Josh in June climbed up on the counter with the block of frozen meat.

"Don't worry. The meat still has to be cooked." Josh in June swung the pickax down.

Clang!

It took a while and made an awful lot of noise, but Josh in June finally managed to break off some pieces of the mealy mystery meat.

Just then the kitchen door opened. It was Principal Blanco!

19

Andy in April and I in May held our breath as Principal Blanco stared at Josh in June standing on the kitchen counter with the pickax.

Finally our principal sighed. "Could you keep it down? I'm getting complaints about the noise."

Josh in June nodded mutely. Principal Blanco left.

"Now I've seen *everything*," Andy in April mumbled.

"No," I said in May's body. "You still haven't seen four hundred starving kids screaming for lunch."

We got back to work. I don't know how we did it, but somehow we managed to get the tacos made just in time.

Briiinnngggg! The lunch bell rang. Almost immediately kids started pouring into the kitchen and sliding trays along the rail. One of the first kids on line was Barry Dunn.

"Hey, lunch lady," he said, "whatcha got?"

"How about a first name," Josh in June's body replied.

"I know your first name," Barry said with a grin. "It's Lunch. And your last name is Lady. Now, how about some grub?"

"My first name happens to be Josh . . . er, I mean, June," Josh in June informed him.

"Yeah, whatever," Barry said. "So gimme lunch."

"Say please," I said in May's body.

"What?" Barry frowned.

I crossed May's tattooed arms. "Haven't you ever heard of asking politely?"

Some of the other kids in line smiled as if they were glad that someone was finally standing up to Barry.

"What is this?" Barry asked.

"It's called manners, Barry," I said in May's body.

Barry scowled at me.

"You're holding up the line, Barry," I said.

Barry turned to Josh in June's body. "Okay, so, uh, could I have lunch, *please*?"

"Of course." Josh in June handed him a plate with a taco on it. Barry slid his tray down to Andy in April's body at the cash register. He pulled a crumpled dollar bill out of his pocket.

"Unfold it, please," I said in May's body.

"*You* unfold it," Barry shot back.

"Step out of line, Barry," I ordered in May's body. "Let the kids who want to pay go ahead."

Barry stepped out of line and stood with his tray while the other kids passed and paid for their lunches.

"This isn't fair," he whined. "I want to pay, too."

"Then pay with money that isn't hiding your latest surprise," I said in May's body.

"Oh, okay." Barry reached into his pocket and produced some uncrumpled bills. He paid Andy in April's body at the cash register and left the kitchen.

Out in the cafetorium a lot of kids were getting their lunches from the Vend-A-Lunch machines. In May's body I walked past a table where Julia Sax was sitting with some of her friends. They were all eating Vend-A-Lunches.

"Uh, excuse me," Julia said. "We just heard what you did to Barry in the lunch line, and we're really glad someone finally put him in his place."

Suddenly I had an idea. "Then it's too bad," I said in May's body.

"What's too bad?" asked Julia.

"That you kids will probably vote for the Vend-A-Lunch machines. Then there won't be any more lunch ladies to put Barry in his place."

Julia looked down at her Vend-A-Lunch and then back at me in May's body. "Gee, I never thought of that."

Just then Howie Jamison ran into the cafetorium. When he saw me, he skidded to a stop and hung his head.

"I know," he said. "I have to practice walking in and out five times."

"No, you don't," I said in May's body. "Just promise that from now on you'll walk."

"Serious?" Howie asked surprised.

"And think about voting against Vend-A-Lunch this afternoon," I added.

"You bet," said Howie.

Amanda Gluck walked past with a sour look on her face.

"What's the problem, Amanda?" I asked in May's body.

"I couldn't find a single peanut butter and jelly sandwich that I liked," she complained.

"Come with me," I said. Together we went into the kitchen, where Josh in June's body was busy serving lunches. Her face was red and her forehead was dotted with perspiration.

"Excuse me, June," I said.

Josh in June wiped her brow. "What is it, Ja . . . I mean, May?"

"Amanda told me she couldn't find a peanut butter and jelly sandwich she was happy with," I said.

Josh in June frowned. "I showed her every single one I had."

I led Amanda to a table with some bread and

70

big jars of peanut butter and jelly. "Suppose we let you make a sandwich exactly the way you like it?"

Amanda's eyes widened with excitement. "This is super!"

"You think the Vend-A-Lunch Corporation would ever let you make your own sandwich?" I asked in May's body.

"No way," said Amanda.

"Remember that when you vote today," I said.

20

Lunch was over. The cafetorium was empty. I went back into the kitchen. Josh in June's body was patting her damp forehead with a paper towel.

"Wow, that's hard work," she said. "Hot, too."

"And some of those kids are so rude." Andy in April opened April's bag. She took out a small makeup case and studied herself in the mirror.

Josh in June turned to me in May. "I hate to say this, Jake, but I think Andy was right. Now that I've been a lunch lady for a day, I can see what they go through."

"You couldn't *pay* me to do this every day," said Andy in April's body. She took a pad out of the makeup case and patted her cheeks with it.

"Uh, Andy?" said Josh in June.

"Hmmm?" Andy in April patted the makeup pad against her chin.

"Mind if I ask what you're doing?" Josh in June asked.

"Just freshening up after lunch," Andy in April replied.

Josh in June's body and I in May's body shared a nervous look.

"Andy," I reminded him. "You're not a lunch lady. You're a kid trapped in a lunch lady's body."

"That doesn't mean that I don't care about my looks," Andy in April replied with a huff as she primped April's big hair.

"The question is, *who* are you trying to look nice for?" I asked in May's body.

"That's right!" said Josh in June. "You're the only one among us who's married."

Andy in April closed the makeup case. "So?"

"So we've got two periods left and then school's over," I said in May's body. "And when school's over I'll have to go home to May's mother."

"And I'll have to go home to Poopsie," said Josh in June.

"And guess who you'll have to go home to?" I asked Andy.

"April's husband!" Our friend gasped.

Josh puckered June's lips. "I bet he'll want to give you a big, wet, welcome-home kiss."

Andy in April's jaw dropped.

"A lot of husbands and wives share the same bathroom," I added.

"Some people even take showers together," said Josh in June's body.

73

I picked up April's pocketbook and started to go through it.

"Just what do you think you're doing?" asked Andy in April's body.

"Looking for this!" I pulled out a photo of a big, hairy man with a bald head and a bushy beard. "Guess who this is?"

Andy in April stared at the photo. "The abominable snowman?"

"No, sweetie cakes," grinned Josh in June. "That's your husband."

21

Andy in April turned pale. "We have to switch back into our own bodies before the abominable snowman tries to plant a wet one on my cheek!"

"We can't," I said in May's body. "Thanks to you the mini-DITS is totally fried. I'm not sure even Mr. Dirksen would know how to fix it."

"That still leaves the big DITS," said Andy in April.

"But it's locked in the science lab," I said in May's body.

"Someone must have a key," said Josh in June.

"Principal Blanco and Mr. Dirksen," I said in May's body.

"Forget that," said Josh in June. "There's no way we'll be able to get the key from Blanco. And Dirksen is still in the Amazon."

"Then it's hopeless," Andy in April moped. "We're gonna be stuck in these bodies until Mr. Dirksen comes back."

The future looked pretty dismal. Maybe April, May, and June liked being lunch ladies, but we sure didn't.

Suddenly, the kitchen door swung open and Jessica rushed in. "April, May, June, I've been looking all over for you!"

"Why?" I asked in May's body.

"Because I did it!" Jessica said excitedly. "I convinced Principal Blanco to have a special Lunch Lady Appreciation Day assembly. It'll be the last period. Just before the vote. The whole school's going to come. This'll be our last chance to convince everyone to vote against Vend-A-Lunch!"

"An assembly?" Andy in April repeated nervously.

"Can't you see it?" asked Jessica. "The three of you up on the stage, sharing all your passion and love for the lunch room. Telling the students everything it means to be a lunch lady!"

"Uh, that sounds really great," said Josh in June's body.

"There's just one problem," added Andy in April.

Jessica scowled. "What?"

I swallowed and cleared May's throat. "We're not the lunch ladies."

22

"**Y**ou're not the . . . " Jessica blinked as she realized what I meant. She knew about the DITS from all the other times I'd switched bodies, including the time I switched bodies with her!

My sister's face hardened. "All right, who's who?"

"I'm Josh," said Josh in June's body.

"I'm Andy," said Andy in April's body.

Jessica turned to me in May's body. "Why, Jake?"

"It's a long story," I answered.

"It was his idea," Josh in June pointed at Andy in April.

"But it was his fault!" Andy in April pointed back at Josh in June.

"That's bull!" yelled Josh in June's body.

"Is not!" shouted Andy in April's body. "If you hadn't been so . . . so *insensitive* about lunch ladies, I never would have switched you. But *noooooo*, you couldn't think about lunch ladies as real people. All *you* could think about were those stupid Vend-A-Lunches."

"All right." Jessica crossed her arms and nodded. "I think I'm starting to get the picture of what happened. Let me ask you something, June, er, I mean, Josh. Now that you've actually experienced what it's like to be a lunch lady, have you changed your mind?"

"Uh . . . " Josh in June's body darted her eyes back and forth.

"Fess up, Josh," Andy in April urged her.

"Yeah, Josh, do it." I nodded May's head in agreement.

"You can't make me say that Mealy Mystery Meat is better than a Vend-A-Burger," Josh in June insisted.

"We're not talking about *food*," Jessica argued. "We're talking about the environment. We're talking about human beings being replaced by a machine. We're talking about people's lives being ruined."

"Couldn't the lunch ladies go to work for the Vend-A-Lunch Corporation?" Josh in June asked.

"Doing what?" asked Andy in April.

"They could go around refilling the machines," suggested Josh in June.

"But then they'd be traveling to a dozen schools a day," Jessica argued. "Where's the personal relationship? Where's the nurturing?"

"How many kids have a personal relationship

with their lunch lady?" Josh in June asked skeptically.

"I did when I went here," answered Jessica.

"You don't count," Josh in June shot back. "You'd have a personal relationship with a speed bump if you could. I meant, who *else* has a personal relationship with a lunch lady?"

"I do," said Andy in April.

"Bull," countered Josh in June. "You've never had a relationship with any of the lunch ladies here."

"Not here," said Andy in April. "But . . . at another school."

Josh in June's body frowned. "But you go to school here."

"I do," Andy in April said. "But my mom works at another school."

"So?" said Josh in June.

Andy in April took a breath and let it out slowly. "She's a lunch lady."

23

We all stared at Andy in April in amazement.

"You never told us that," I said in May's body.

"You always said she was a brain surgeon," said Josh in June's body.

"I know." Andy nodded April's big head of black hair sadly. "I was afraid you'd make fun of me if I told you the truth."

Jessica put her arm around April's shoulders. "Oh, April."

"Andy," Andy in April's body corrected her.

"Right, Andy," Jessica said. "That's so touching."

"For all these years I thought your mother was using one of those cool little saws to cut open people's heads," grumbled Josh in June. "Now I find out all she did was serve lunch."

"Is the Vend-A-Lunch Corporation trying to replace the lunch ladies at her school?" I asked in May's body.

"No," said Andy in April.

"You mean, *not yet*," my sister corrected her. "But what do you think will happen if we let them keep the Vend-A-Lunch machines here? It'll spread. Maybe not this year, but next year or the year after. It's the domino theory."

"What's the domino theory?" asked Josh in June.

"You know how you can stand up a bunch of dominoes in a row, then knock one down, and they all fall?" Jessica asked.

"What's that got to do with lunch ladies?" asked Andy in April.

"It's the same thing," said Jessica.

"They're gonna line up all the lunch ladies and knock them down?" asked Josh in June.

"No!" Jessica cried. "Think of our school as a domino."

Josh in June scratched her head. "They're gonna line up *schools* and knock them down?"

"Cool!" grinned Andy in April.

"No!" Jessica shook her head. "What I'm trying to say is that if Burt Ipchupt Middle School falls this year, Andy's mom's school may fall next year."

Josh in June made a face. "Gee, they must be really far apart."

"What are you talking about?" Jessica asked.

"Well, if you're gonna line up all these schools and one is gonna fall into the next," Josh in June explained, "and Burp It Up is going to fall *this* year, but Andy's mom's school isn't supposed to fall until *next* year, then they must be really far apart. Like Burp It Up must be at the front of the line and Andy's mom's school must be way at the back."

"Or maybe because schools are a lot bigger they fall a lot slower than lunch ladies," Andy in April mused.

"But doesn't your mom go to work and come home every day?" I asked Andy in April's body.

"Yes," she replied.

"Then they can't be *that* far apart," I said in May's body.

"They're not," said Andy in April. "She works in Middletown."

Jessica blinked. "Does anyone know what we're talking about?"

"How long it takes my mom to get to work?" Andy in April guessed.

"Schools falling into each other?" guessed June in Josh.

"Lunch ladies falling into each other?" I guessed in May's body.

"Okay, forget the domino theory," Jessica said.

"Aw, that's no fair!" Andy in April whined.

"Yeah," I agreed in May's body. "We were just getting into it."

"You think the domino theory would work with school principals, too?" Josh in June wondered.

"*Shut up!*" Jessica screamed.

We fell into a shocked silence.

"What's with you?" I finally asked.

"We've gotten totally off the track," said Jessica.

"What track?" asked Andy in April.

"*Stop it!*" Jessica shouted. "I mean it. This is serious. Now, before we got sidetracked, Andy — "

"I thought we were totally *off* the track," said Josh in June.

"We were, but now we're just sidetracked," Andy in April informed her.

"Right," said Jessica. "And now we're getting back on track."

"The same track or a different track?" I asked in May's body.

Jessica's face turned red and her eyes started to bulge. She reached toward my neck like she wanted to strangle me in May's body.

"Okay, okay!" I backed away in May's body. "Just stay on track."

"Right." Jessica nodded and turned to Andy in April's body. "Your mom is a lunch lady so you understand how the lunch ladies here must feel about losing their jobs."

"True," Andy in April agreed.

"So you'll go to the assembly and tell the students how much you love them and how important it is that you have a personal relationship with them?" Jessica asked.

My friends and I shared a nervous look in our lunch lady bodies.

"Do we *have* to?" I asked in May's body.

"If you don't, who will?" Jessica asked.

"How about the real lunch ladies?" asked Josh in June.

"That would help," Jessica replied. "But the real lunch ladies aren't here. They're off in your bodies somewhere."

Josh in June's body looked up at the clock. "Actually, right now they should be in Mr. Grout's class."

"We better go find them and tell them the plan," Jessica said.

"You'll have to go," I said in May's body. "We can't. Every time Blanco catches us in the hall he sends us back here."

"All right," my sister said. "You stay here. I'll go get them."

"That won't be necessary," said Andy in April.

Jessica stopped. "Why not?"

"Because they're not in Mr. Grout's class." Our friend pointed out one of the lunchroom windows. Outside, May, the lunch lady in my body, was bouncing across the football field . . . on the Kazubi dirt bike.

And April in Andy's body was sitting on the back.

24

"**I** don't believe it!" Jessica gasped.

Josh in June turned to me in May's body. "I didn't know you could drive a dirt bike, Jake."

"I can't," I replied. "That's May in my body."

"Know what'll happen if Blanco sees that?" asked Andy in April.

"We'll be expelled!" I gasped in May's body.

"That sounds a little harsh," said Jessica. "I'd bet on a week's suspension."

"No, Blanco told us this morning that if he caught us doing one more thing wrong, he'd expel us," I explained in May's body. "It's the straw that broke the camel's back."

"I still say it was a cinder block," said Andy in April.

"I still vote for the cement mixer," countered Josh in June.

"Why would a camel carry a cement mixer?" Jessica asked.

"Yeah." Andy nodded in April's body. "That's what I said."

"Excuse me, folks. Aren't we getting off the track?" I asked in May's body.

"What would a camel be doing on a track?" asked Andy in April.

"Maybe it's practicing for the camel decathlon," proposed Josh in June.

"With a cement mixer on its back?" asked Jessica.

"One of the events could be weight lifting," Andy in April speculated.

We were all quiet for a moment as we tried to imagine a camel running around a track and trying to lift a cement mixer.

"Exactly *how* would a camel lift a cement mixer anyway?" Josh in June finally asked.

"Very carefully," I answered in May's body. "But seriously, guys. If Principal Blanco sees those two lunch ladies in our bodies riding across the football field on a dirt bike, we are gonna be toast."

"*Burned* toast," added Andy in April.

"You're right! That could ruin everything!" Jessica headed for the exit. "We have to stop them!"

The next thing I knew, we were all running toward the football field, waving and shouting. Luckily, May in my body saw us and stopped the dirt bike.

"What do you think you're doing?" Jessica asked as she ran up to the dirt bike.

"I'm not who you think I am," warned May in my body as she straddled the dirt bike in my gym clothes. Small clouds of white exhaust smoke puffed out of the dirt bike's tailpipe.

"I know," said Jessica. "You're May the lunch lady in my brother's body."

May raised my eyebrow. "He's your brother?"

"Yes," said Jessica. "And he's going to be in huge trouble if Principal Blanco sees him riding around here on a dirt bike."

"Told you so," said April in Andy's body from the back of the bike.

"But I always wanted to do this," May in my body said with a pout.

"Is that really your bike?" I asked in her body.

May nodded my head.

"You ride it to school every day?" asked Andy in April's body.

"Yes," answered May in my body.

"That's pretty cool for a lunch lady," said Andy in April's body.

"Hon, I really don't like what you're doing with my hair," said April in Andy to Andy in April.

Andy in April touched her big black hair self-consciously. "I was afraid you might say that. But I don't know your tricks."

"You have to tease it out," explained April in Andy. "Here, I'll show you."

April in Andy got off the dirt bike, pulled a

comb out of Andy's pocket, and went to work on April's hair.

"See how you do it?" April in Andy asked as he teased the lunch lady's hair.

"I think so," said Andy in April's body. "Let me try."

Andy in April took the comb and started to tease her hair.

"You can use the dirt bike's mirror," April in Andy suggested.

"Good idea." Andy in April bent down and peered into the mirror as she teased her hair.

"That's it!" April in Andy nodded approvingly. "Now you're getting it!"

Smiling proudly, Andy in April turned to me in May's body and Josh in June's body. "See, guys? Now I know how to tease out hair."

"I'm so thrilled," muttered Josh in June.

"Listen," said Jessica. "I hate to interrupt this little hair and makeup party, but if you lunch ladies want to keep your jobs, we have a lot of work to do."

"What about getting our bodies back?" asked April in Andy.

"Uh, we'll try to work on that, too," said Jessica. "But first we better get back into school before someone sees us."

"Hey, wait a minute!" said Josh in June's body. Where's June in my body?"

25

I noticed that May in my body and April in Andy's body shared a look. Josh in June noticed it, too.

"I saw that!" said Josh in June. "So where is she?"

Instead of answering, May in my body and April in Andy's body glanced over at the gym. The gym door opened and June in Josh's body trotted out . . . carrying a long pole.

"Pole vault?" Josh in June sputtered.

April nodded Andy's head. "It's all she's ever wanted to do."

"We have to stop her!" Jessica gasped. My sister started to run, but May in my body grabbed her arm.

"Let her do it," the lunch lady in my body said.

"But the assembly!" Jessica cried.

"It can wait," said April in Andy.

"I don't understand," my sister moaned.

"It's a once-in-a-lifetime opportunity," said May in my body.

"A dream come true," added April in Andy.

"It could cost you your jobs," argued Jessica.

"Some things are worth the risk," answered May in my body.

"What is life without hope?" asked April in Andy.

"But why pole-vaulting?" asked Jessica.

"Why ride a dirt bike?" replied May in my body.

"Why tease your hair?" asked April in Andy.

"They're right!" Andy in April suddenly realized. "It's why I had to try to ride my BMX backward with Josh and Jake standing on the grind pegs!"

"Want to know what keeps us lunch ladies going?" asked April in Andy.

"Free leftovers?" guessed Josh in June.

"No." May shook my head. "Hopes and dreams."

My sister's eyes began to glisten with tears. "That's . . . that's so touching!"

By now, June in Josh's body reached the pole-vault pit. We watched as he put up the bar and then walked slowly back down the runway.

"Does anyone care that I've never pole-vaulted in my life?" asked Josh in June.

"No!" we all answered at once.

We watched in silence as June in Josh stopped

at the beginning of the runway and lifted the pole.

"Everyone cross your fingers," Jessica whispered, and wiped a tear from her eye.

We all crossed our fingers.

Over on the runway, June in Josh took a deep breath and began to run.

"Uh, folks?" I whispered in May's body.

"Shush!" Jessica shushed me.

"But this is *important*!" I hissed.

"It can wait," grumbled April in Andy.

"I don't think so," I said.

"Why? What's wrong?" asked May in my body.

By now, June in Josh was halfway down the runway and running as hard as he could.

"Well, you know how pole-vault pits always have those thick mats to land on?" I asked in May's body.

My question hung in the air for a moment.

"Oh, my gosh!" April in Andy gasped. "There's nothing for her to land on!"

26

All at once we started to run.

"Stop!" April in Andy shouted at June in Josh.

"That's *my* body she's going to destroy!" Josh in June panted as she tried to keep up with the rest of us.

But we were too late. June in Josh's body reached the end of the runway. The pole slid into the ground and started to bend. June in Josh gripped the other end of the pole tightly.

Suddenly, he began to lift into the air!

Higher!

Higher!

The pole straightened out.

June in Josh's body vaulted upward and let go!

The lunch lady in our friend's body flew even higher into the air!

He cleared the bar!

Then shot downward like a stone.

And crashed to the ground with a loud *thud*.

27

June in Josh's body lay motionless on the ground. His eyes were closed.

"My body!" Josh in June cried.

May in my body and April in Andy were the first to get there. They fell to their knees next to June in Josh.

"Is he breathing?" April in Andy gasped.

May in my body pressed my ear close to June in Josh's mouth. "I think so."

I arrived in May's body, followed by Andy in April.

"What should we do?" I asked.

May in my body slapped June in Josh gently on the cheek. "June? Can you hear me? June?"

June in Josh didn't respond. He just lay there with his eyes closed.

Josh in June lumbered up. "I knew it! She gave me a concussion! She broke my neck!"

"Be quiet!" May in my body snapped. She slapped June in Josh's cheek a little harder.

"Come on, hon. Wake up. You have to wake up!"

June in Josh didn't budge.

"Oh, no!" Josh in June cried. "I'm dead!"

"No, you're not," said April in Andy.

"You're right!" Josh in June gasped. "It's worse than death! I'll be stuck in June's body forever! I'll have to be a lunch lady! I'll have to go home at night and change Poopsie's kitty litter!"

Suddenly June opened Josh's eyes. "Did someone say Poopsie?"

"June?" May in my body cried. "You're okay?"

"I . . . I think so," answered June in Josh.

"Oh, June, we were so worried." May in my body put my arms around June in Josh's body and hugged him.

My friends and I watched in shock.

"Uh, guys?" Josh in June said.

"Leave them alone," warned Jessica. "Can't you see that this is an important moment?"

"Well, sure," I said in May's body. "Only if anyone in school is watching this, they're seeing Josh Hopka and Jake Sherman rolling around on the ground hugging each other."

"So?" Jessica challenged me. "Can't two boys hug each other in joy?"

"Not in middle school," I grumbled in May's body.

"Not in *any* school," added Josh in June.

Jessica gave us a disgusted look. "Haven't you two learned *anything*?"

94

"Sure," answered Josh in June. "I've learned to always check for proper padding before pole-vaulting."

"I've learned that being a lunch lady doesn't mean you can't drive a dirt bike," I said in May's body.

"I've learned that a female pigeon can't lay an egg unless it sees another pigeon or looks at itself in a mirror," added Andy in April.

Still kneeling next to June in Josh, May in my body looked up. "Do pigeons really carry mirrors?"

"Hey," said Andy in April, "if a camel can carry a cement mixer, why not?"

"Why would a camel carry a cement mixer?" asked April in Andy.

"Please!" Jessica begged. "Don't start this again! We have to get back to school. The assembly's going to begin any minute now."

We helped June in Josh to his feet and headed back toward school. May in my body walked the dirt bike. Jessica told the lunch ladies in our bodies about the assembly and how this would be their last chance to save their jobs.

We got back to school and left the dirt bike by the kitchen door. In the hallway outside the cafetorium Cathy was sitting at a desk with a petition on a clipboard. Howie Jamison and Ollie Hawkins were signing it.

"Look! More kids have signed!" Cathy called

when she saw us coming. She held up the petition. Half of one page was covered with signatures.

"That's all we've got?" Jessica asked.

"It's better than before," said Cathy.

"But it's still nowhere near enough," Jessica said. "We need pages and pages of signatures. We need a *majority* of the students to vote for the lunch ladies."

"I'll keep trying," Cathy promised.

Just then the school loudspeaker blared: *"All students to the cafetorium for the assembly."*

"This is it!" Jessica gasped. She turned to the lunch ladies in our bodies and my friends and me in the lunch lady bodies. "Okay, everyone, this is our last chance to save the lunch ladies. I'll go first and make an opening statement. Who wants to go next?"

My friends and I in the lunch lady bodies looked at the lunch ladies in our bodies.

"I guess we should go next," said May in my body.

"I was hoping you'd say that," said Jessica. "Just remember. Everyone will think you're Josh, Andy, and Jake. You'll have a huge advantage because you'll seem like three ordinary kids who normally couldn't care less about lunch ladies. This is your chance to convince them."

"What about us?" asked Andy in April's body.

"I'm sorry, April, er, I mean, Andy," my sister said, "but everyone's going to think you're just lunch ladies. They *expect* you to want to keep your jobs. I can't imagine that the students here will really care about what you have to say."

Kids began to enter the hallway on their way to the cafetorium. Jessica turned to the lunch ladies in our bodies. "Okay, ladies, er, I mean, boys, it's time to go."

"Wait!" I said in May's body. "What are we supposed to do?"

"Why are you asking Jessica Sherman?" a voice asked.

We turned. Principal Blanco was standing in the hall behind us.

"Why aren't you in the kitchen?" he asked my friends and me in the lunch lady bodies.

"Well, uh, we finished serving lunch," Josh in June replied.

"Then you should be preparing *tomorrow's* lunch," Principal Blanco said.

"But — " Andy in April began to argue, but I grabbed her arm.

"Come on, April, deary," I said in May's body. "Let's go."

28

My friends and I in the lunch lady bodies started down the hall toward the cafetorium.

"I don't want to make tomorrow's lunch," Andy in April muttered. "I — "

"Chill out," I whispered in May's body as we went into the kitchen. "We're not going to make tomorrow's lunch."

"Then what — " began Josh in June.

"We're going to stay in here and listen," I whispered, pushing the kitchen door open an inch and peeking out into the cafetorium.

The cafetorium was filled with kids. My friends and I watched as Principal Blanco climbed onto the stage and got everyone's attention.

"All right, students, quiet down. We are now going to have a public debate concerning the lunch lady versus Vend-A-Lunch issue. At the end of the debate, we will have the vote. First,

Jessica Sherman will speak on behalf of the lunch ladies."

Jessica stepped up to the microphone and made her plea to keep the lunch ladies and get rid of the Vend-A-Lunch machines.

The crowd listened quietly.

Then the lunch ladies in our bodies spoke.

Again, the crowd listened quietly.

When the lunch ladies in our bodies were finished, Principal Blanco went up to the microphone again.

"So far we have heard from people in favor of keeping the lunch ladies," he said. "But to make this a fair debate we should hear from the other side as well. Does anyone have anything to say in favor of the Vend-A-Lunch machines?"

Alex Silver raised his hand and went up on stage.

"I think the Vend-A-Lunch machines really rule," he told the audience. "The food's a hundred times better and those machines can't make you pick up five pieces of garbage every time you drop something on the cafetorium floor."

"*Yeah!*" For the first time during the debate the crowd cheered.

In the school kitchen, my friends and I in the lunch lady bodies shared a dismal look.

"It doesn't look good for the lunch ladies," Josh in June mumbled.

Alex Silver stepped down and Principal Blanco asked if anyone else wanted to speak. Barry Dunn raised his hand and went up to the stage.

The crowd began to whisper loudly. Barry Dunn usually didn't care about anything. No one could imagine what he would have to say about the lunch ladies.

Barry stood on the stage with a funny smile on his face. He waited until the crowd quieted down. Then he leaned toward the microphone.

"This is what I think of school." He put his hand into his armpit and made a loud, disgusting sound.

The crowd started to laugh and cheer. Principal Blanco stormed across the stage and grabbed Barry's collar. "That's it, Dunn. You're going straight to the office."

Mr. Rope, the gym teacher, took over the debate. Most of the kids who went up to the stage spoke in favor of the Vend-A-Lunch machines.

A little while later, Principal Blanco came back and took over the debate again.

"Does anyone else have anything to say concerning the issue of Vend-A-Lunch or lunch lady lunch?" he asked through the microphone.

Murmurs and whispers rippled through the crowd, but no one raised a hand. In the school kitchen, my friends and I shared a disappointed glance.

"Looks bad for the lunch ladies," Andy in April said, tugging nervously at her hair.

"*Really* bad," I said in May's body.

"We have to do something to get the kids on our side," said Andy in April.

"Like what?" Josh in June asked.

"Let's think about this," said Andy in April. "What's the real problem we're facing here?"

"Vend-A-Lunches taste better than lunch lady lunches," Josh in June said.

"*Besides that*," Andy in April grumbled.

"Kids still don't care about lunch ladies," I said in May's body. "They still think they're just a bunch of dork-a-zoids."

"Then we have to change their minds," Andy in April said.

"Impossible," argued Josh in June. "There's no time left. They're going to start voting in a couple of minutes."

Andy in April slammed her fist into her hand. "We have to convince them that lunch ladies are cool."

"How?" I asked in May's body.

Andy in April looked around. "I've got it!"

29

"**I** can't believe I'm doing this," Josh in June muttered as she climbed onto May's dirt bike behind Andy in April.

"Are you *sure* you know how to drive one of these things?" I asked in May's body.

"Nope," replied Andy in April. "But how different from a BMX bike can it be?"

"A *lot* different," Josh in June said.

Andy in April ignored her. "You know what to do, Jake?"

I nodded May's head. I knew what Andy wanted me to do. I just couldn't quite believe that I was going to do it.

"You better get going," Andy in April said.

I left the kitchen and went out into the cafetorium. Principal Blanco was still standing at the microphone. "All right, everyone, since no one has anything more to say on the issue, we will now have a vote. We'll start with the — "

"Wait!" I yelled in May's body and hurried onto the stage.

"What do you want, May?" Principal Blanco asked.

"I want a chance to speak in favor of the lunch ladies," I said in May's body.

Principal Blanco sighed. "Very well, but hurry. School's going to be over soon and we still haven't voted."

I stepped up to the microphone and looked out at the crowd. The cafetorium was filled with kids. A few were my friends, but a lot of them were just faces with no names. In the front row, my sister, Jessica, nodded at me and pumped her fist in support. I could feel May's heart start to pound in her, I mean, my chest. I cleared her throat nervously.

"Well, er, I guess you're all wondering why I'm standing here," I began. "Well, it's because there are things about lunch ladies that you don't know about. And I think you should know about them before you vote. For instance, I bet you didn't know that being a lunch lady is cool."

A couple of kids in the audience groaned. Even Jessica rolled her eyes. In May's body I glanced at the kitchen door, wondering where Andy was. Meanwhile, Principal Blanco stood on the side of the stage, looking at his watch and tapping his foot impatiently.

"And here's another thing," I went on. "I bet you didn't know that some lunch ladies can recite the alphabet in reverse. Like this: Z, Y, X, W, V, U . . ."

"Boo!" "Get off the stage!" "Get a life!" Kids in the audience began to shout and jeer. Principal Blanco started across the stage toward me.

I looked at the kitchen door again. *Where was Andy?*

Vrrrrooooom!

Everyone in the cafetorium swiveled their heads as Andy in April's body shot out of the kitchen on the dirt bike with Josh in June's body on the back. The bike left a trail of white exhaust smoke.

"What in the world?" Principal Blanco cried.

"Here's another excellent example of what makes lunch ladies cool," I yelled through the microphone as Andy in April drove the dirt bike up the aisle toward the steps leading to the stage. "Lunch ladies ride dirt bikes!"

I expected Andy in April to stop the bike at the steps, but instead she hit the steps and started to ride up them!

"Lunch ladies do dirt bike stunts!" I shouted into the microphone.

Still riding the dirt bike, Andy in April and Josh in June made it onto the stage.

"You can't drive that thing up here!" Principal Blanco yelled and waved his arms, but Andy in April drove right past him.

"What took you so long?" I asked in May's body.

"I couldn't get the darn thing started!" Andy in April yelled back as she started to circle the stage on the dirt bike.

In May's body I turned back to the microphone and shouted, "Lunch ladies go where no one has dared to go before!"

"Get that thing off the stage!" Principal Blanco yelled, and ran after the dirt bike. Meanwhile, the stage was starting to cloud over with exhaust smoke.

"Jump on the front!" Andy in April yelled as she passed me.

"But you've never done three!" I gasped in May's body.

"There's always a first time!" Andy in April yelled back.

I yanked the microphone off the stand and jumped onto the front of the dirt bike.

"Lunch ladies perform death-defying feats!" I announced to the crowd.

"Yeah!" "All right!" "Way cool!" The crowd clapped and cheered.

"Come back here!" Principal Blanco wheezed and coughed on the exhaust smoke as he chased us around the stage.

"I think we better listen to him," Josh in June yelled from the back of the dirt bike.

"You're right," said Andy in April. She stopped

the dirt bike and we got off. We were on one side of the stage and Principal Blanco was on the other. He was bent over, trying to catch his breath.

"You want this dirt bike?" Andy in April asked.

"Yes." Principal Blanco nodded.

"It's all yours." Andy in April revved the engine, clicked the bike into gear, and sent it across the stage.

Principal Blanco's eyes widened in terror as the dirt bike shot toward him. He held out his hands and tried to stop it by grabbing the handlebars, but it went right past him and yanked him onto the seat!

The next thing we knew, Principal Blanco was on the dirt bike and bouncing down the steps of the stage.

"Whoa! Look out! Yeow! Help! Watch it!"

The dirt bike hit the bottom step and shot through the cafetorium, with Principal Blanco barely able to hold on. It disappeared into the hallway, leaving only a white cloud of exhaust.

30

It was time to switch back to our own bodies. Everyone hurried down the hall to the science lab.

"This is ridiculous!" Josh in June sputtered and panted as she ran. "We'll never be able to get into Mr. Dirksen's lab. You've seen the padlock Blanco put on the door."

"Doesn't matter," I replied in May's body. "We have to get in there. It's our only chance."

"If that's our only chance, we might as well forget it," Josh panted.

"No way!" cried Andy in April. "Jake's right! We have to try! We might be able to pry the door open with a crowbar."

"We don't have a crowbar," May in my body replied.

"Then we'll knock the hinges off with a sledgehammer," Andy said.

"No sledgehammer, either," said April in Andy.

"Then we'll drill through with an electric drill," Andy said.

"With what drill?" asked June in Josh.

"Okay, okay," said Andy. "We'll *blow* the door open with dynamite."

"Give me a break," Josh groaned.

"Okay, okay." Andy in April reached the science lab door and put her hand on the door knob. "Then we'll . . . we'll *turn the knob and push it open.*"

Andy in April turned the doorknob.

The door swung open.

My friends and I stared at the open door.

"I don't get it," said Josh in June.

April in Andy poked his head in. "There's someone in there."

31

We all looked in. A man with a long, shaggy beard was bent over the big DITS. He was wearing a hat with a floppy brim, and his shirt and pants were covered with rips and stains. His skin was darkly tanned. A large backpack with a sleeping bag lay in the corner, but the man ignored it. He had opened the back of the DITS and was busy with the wires and circuit boards inside.

"Uh, excuse me," I said in May's body.

The man straightened up and looked surprised.

"How did you get in here?" asked Andy in April's body.

"I used a key," the man answered. His voice sounded vaguely familiar.

"Where did you get a key?" asked Josh in June's body.

The man scowled. "Jake Sherman, Josh Hopka, Andy Kent, and three lunch ladies. I don't mean to be rude, but what are *you* doing here and why are *you* asking me these questions?"

Now I recognized that voice. "Mr. Dirksen!"

The hairy man nodded. "That's right."

"When did you get back from the Amazon?" I asked in May's body.

"Just now," our science teacher replied. "Why are you all here?"

Josh in June, Andy in April, and I in May shared a look.

"Well, you see," I began, "we're not really lunch ladies."

Mr. Dirksen blinked, then turned to the lunch ladies in our bodies. "Let me take a wild guess," he said to them. "You're not really students?"

The lunch ladies in our bodies nodded.

The lines in Mr. Dirksen's darkly tanned forehead deepened. "Which one of you is really Jake Sherman?"

I sheepishly raised May's hand.

"I entrusted the mini-DITS to you, Jake," Mr. Dirksen said with great seriousness. "You promised me you would keep it safe and not use it. Now I come back and discover that you and your friends have all switched bodies with lunch ladies."

In the lunch lady bodies, my friends and I shared a guilty look.

"Please tell me that this has been the only time you've violated my trust," Mr. Dirksen said.

I didn't know what to say.

"Well?" Mr. Dirksen said impatiently.

"Uh, you see, I, er . . . "

"There have been *other* times?" he asked, raising both eyebrows.

"Not . . . *that* many," I said in May's body.

"Just once, I hope," said Mr. Dirksen.

"Let's see." Josh in June started counting on her fingers. "Our counselor at Camp Grimley."

"And we turned that other counselor, Axel, into a rock," Andy added.

"A rock!" Mr. Dirksen repeated in disbelief.

"And I switched with Principal Blanco," said Josh in June.

"And you can't forget Erie Lake," Andy in April reminded me.

"The movie star?" Mr. Dirksen realized. "Who did he switch with?"

"Let's see," said Andy in April. "Jake, Josh, and Principal Blanco."

Mr. Dirksen pursed his lips and turned to me. "I'm very disappointed in you, Jake. I demand that you return the mini-DITS to me immediately."

In May's body I swallowed nervously. "Well, er, I'd really like to, but you see, Mr. Dirksen, the mini-DITS sort of got — "

"Nuked," said Josh in June.

For a moment, Mr. Dirksen said nothing. I was relieved that he didn't throw a fit.

"Perhaps it's for the best," he finally said. "I

111

can always build another one. And in the mean-time, you ladies, er, I mean, boys, won't be able to use it to get into any more trouble."

"So tell us about the Amazon," I said in May's body, hoping to change the subject.

A gleam appeared in Mr. Dirksen's eyes. "Better than *tell* you, I'll *show* you."

He went over to the backpack and undid the straps.

"I have solved one of science's greatest mysteries," he said as he reached into the backpack.

"Why our noses run, but our feet smell?" Andy in April guessed hopefully.

"No," answered Mr. Dirksen.

"Why we park in driveways, but drive on parkways?" guessed Josh in June.

"Sorry." Mr. Dirksen shook his head.

"Then what?" I asked.

"This." Mr. Dirksen pulled out something that looked like a head with a face. But it was the size of a softball. "How to shrink heads!"

32

"**E**eeew!" "Disgusting!" In our bodies, the lunch ladies groaned and moaned.

In the lunch lady bodies, my friends and I all stared at the shrunken head, fascinated.

"Is that real?" Andy in April asked.

"Yes," answered Mr. Dirksen.

"Cool!" gasped Josh in June.

"How'd you get it?" I asked in May's body.

"I bet you just chopped some guy's head off, right?" said Josh in June. "Then shrank that sucker down."

"Of course not," Mr. Dirksen replied. "This poor fellow lost his head in a car accident. But the good news is that I've improved on the technology. Shrinking heads used to be a dirty, messy job involving lots of nasty chemicals. I've figured out how to do it electronically."

Our science teacher picked up his screwdriver and turned back to the DITS.

"Wait a minute!" I gasped in May's body. "What are you doing?"

"I'm reconfiguring the Dirksen Intelligence Transfer System into Dirksen's Unique Negating Cranium Effector."

"From the DITS to the DUNCE?" I said in May's body. My friends and I in our lunch lady bodies shared a worried look.

"You mean, it's not going to be the DITS anymore?" Andy in April asked nervously.

"That's right," answered Mr. Dirksen. "Let's face it. The DITS never worked correctly. It was supposed to transfer intelligence between people. But all it ever did was make them switch bodies."

"There's just one problem," I pointed out. "If you reconfigure the DITS into the DUNCE, we'll be stuck in these bodies forever."

Mr. Dirksen paused from his work and nodded thoughtfully. "The history of science is littered with human sacrifice. Look at it this way, boys. There are worse things than being lunch ladies."

"I beg your pardon," huffed May in my body. "Just who do you think you are?"

"That's right," added April in Andy. "It just so happens my husband needs me to cook his dinner tonight."

"And I have to take care of Poopsie," added June in Josh.

"Who's Poopsie?" asked Mr. Dirksen.

"My kitty," answered June in Josh. "And do

you know what will happen if I come home looking like a teenage boy? Poopsie will be very, very — "

He was interrupted by the sound of a motor-cycle coming down the hall.

"Whoa! Look out! Help!" Still on the dirt bike, Principal Blanco sped through the lab door and headed straight toward the DITS/DUNCE.

Crash!
Whump!
Bang!
Thwunk!

33

The science lab was filled with a smoky haze so thick that I couldn't see my hands in front of my face.

"Is everyone okay?" I called.

"I think so," someone answered in the fog.

"I'm okay."

Then I heard footsteps and the sound of a door creaking open and slamming closed.

"Who was that?" I asked.

"Don't know," answered someone else.

"Sounded like they were in a hurry," said a third person.

The fog and smoke in the lab slowly began to thin. Through the mist, I recognized June.

"Josh, that you?" I asked.

"No, I'm June," she answered.

June? I stared down at the body I was in. The hands I was looking at were mine! I felt my head. It was mine! I was wearing my gym clothes!

"I've switched back!" I realized.

"Me, too!" yelled Andy as the mist lifted some more and I could see him.

"And me," said May.

As the fog continued to thin, we saw Josh and April. They were back in their bodies, too. And now we could see the DITS/DUNCE with the dirt bike smashed into it. It was a wreck.

"Mr. Dirksen?" I said.

"Huh?" a groggy voice came from behind the destroyed machine.

"You okay?" I asked.

"I . . . I'm not sure," he said.

"Is something wrong?" asked June.

"My head," Mr. Dirksen answered. "It feels very, very tight."

A moment later our science teacher stood up.

He looked exactly like he did before the crash.

Only his head was the size of a softball.

"*Ahhhhhhhhh!*" April screamed.

34

"**T**he particles of exhaust smoke from the dirt bike must have become ionized in the crash," Mr. Dirksen was saying.

The rest of us tried to listen to his explanation of what had happened without giggling. It wasn't easy because every time we looked at his softball-sized head we wanted to laugh.

"The ionized particles would have spread the electrical charge throughout the cloud of smoke and fog," Mr. Dirksen continued.

"So you're saying that everyone in the room would be affected," Andy guessed.

"Exactly," said Mr. Dirksen.

"But why didn't it shrink our heads, too?" I asked.

"I'm not sure," answered our science teacher. "My best guess is that because you were in the wrong bodies, your bodies were more inclined to switch than shrink."

"Just one last question," said Andy. "Where's Principal Blanco?"

"Those must have been the footsteps we heard," I said.

"Where would he be in such a hurry to go?" asked Mr. Dirksen.

"The cafetorium!" April cried. "To see what the vote is!"

35

The cafetorium was still filled with students. The curtain in front of the stage was closed. The only thing on the stage was the microphone on the stand.

"What are they waiting for?" I asked as my friends and I joined the crowd.

"They're counting the votes," answered Julia Sax.

The curtains parted and Principal Blanco stepped out.

The crowd went silent with shock.

Like our science teacher's, the principal's head was the size of a softball!

Shocked gasps and murmurs began to ripple through the crowd.

Principal Blanco raised his hands to calm them. "Now, now, students, it's all right. There's no need for panic. There's just been a slight accident."

"I guess we'll never be able to say Principal

Blanco has a swelled head," Amber Sweeny quipped.

Principal Blanco held up an envelope. "I have the results of the vote. As all of you know, the issue of the Vend-A-Lunch versus the lunch ladies has become very heated. Feelings run very strong on both sides. Before I open this envelope and read the results, I need you to promise me that you will accept the decision peacefully no matter which side wins."

The crowd nodded.

"All right, then." Principal Blanco tore open the envelope and read the piece of paper inside. Even though his head was half its normal size, I could see the lines in his brow deepen.

"Well, this is a surprise," he muttered to himself.

"What's the result?" someone in the crowd shouted.

"Tell us!" yelled someone else.

Principal Blanco turned to the microphone. "According to this, the vote . . . is tied."

More gasps and murmurs rippled through the crowd.

"Are you *sure*?" someone yelled.

"Is there anyone who didn't vote?" called someone else.

"What do we do now?" shouted a third.

Principal Blanco scratched his semishrunken head. "Well, to be honest, I don't know."

Suddenly I realized something and yelled, "Wait! There's one person left who hasn't voted!"

"Who?" asked Principal Blanco.

"Barry Dunn."

Principal Blanco blinked his semishrunken eyes. "You're right, Jake. Go get him."

36

I was running down the hall to the office when the bell rang. The school day was over. I pushed open the office door. Barry was just starting to get up.

"Principal Blanco wants you to come to the cafetorium," I said.

Barry shook his head. "Forget it. School's over. I'm out of here."

"No, you're not, Barry," said white-haired Mrs. Hub. "Principal Blanco said you're to serve a week of detention after school here in the office. And if he wants you in the cafetorium, that's where you'll go."

Barry wrinkled his nose at her but followed me into the hall and back to the cafetorium. By the time we got there, most of the school had gone home. Only two small groups remained. On one side of the cafetorium was the pro–Vend-A-Lunch crowd. The other side was the pro–lunch lady group. Both sides yelled at Barry as he walked toward the stage.

"Vote for Vend-A-Lunch!" shouted the pro–Vend-A-Lunch crowd.

"Vote for the lunch ladies!" screamed the pro–lunch lady group.

Barry scowled at both sides, then climbed up onto the stage. When he saw our principal's shrunken head, he blinked with surprise. "Gee, Principal Blanco, what happened to your head?"

"Don't worry about that now, Barry, we have bigger things to deal with," Principal Blanco replied.

"Well, sure," Barry agreed. "Just about *anything* would have to be bigger than your head."

Principal Blanco smirked. "Very funny, Barry. Now, would you mind if we continued?"

"Okay, but would *you* mind if I called you Principal Shrinko instead of Blanco?" Barry asked.

Principal Blanco gritted his teeth. "Yes, I *would* mind." He switched on the microphone so that the whole cafetorium could hear. Everyone grew quiet.

"Do you know why you're here, Barry?" Principal Blanco said through the microphone.

Barry shook his head.

"The entire school has voted on the Vend-A-Lunch versus lunch lady issue," Principal Blanco explained. "The vote is even. You are the only student in school who has not voted. So your vote will decide the issue."

Down on the pro–lunch lady side of the cafetorium, Josh, Andy, and I shared a worried look.

"I guess you could say that this is the vote that broke the camel's back," I whispered.

"That's ridiculous," sputtered Andy. "How much could a vote weigh?"

"It could be a very weighty vote," observed Josh.

Up on the stage, Barry frowned. "You mean, it's up to me to decide whether we keep the Vend-A-Lunch machines or go back to the old lunch lady way?"

Principal Blanco nodded his shrunken head.

"Well . . . " Barry Dunn rubbed his chin and thought. "I hate to say it, but the food from the Vend-A-Lunch machines does taste better."

"Ya-hoo!" cheered the pro–Vend-A-Lunch crowd.

"On the other hand," Barry went on, "I can always steal extra food from the lunch ladies."

"Yeah!" cried the pro–lunch lady group.

"On the *other* hand," Barry continued, "the Vend-A-Breakfast machine means I can eat breakfast here, too."

"Go! Go! Go!" shouted the pro–Vend-A-Lunch crowd.

"On the *other* hand . . . " Barry was still going. "Sometimes I get the lunch lady lunches for free."

"Way to go!" yelled the pro–lunch lady group.

"So what's your decision, Barry?" asked Principal Blanco impatiently.

Barry tugged at his earlobe. "It's a tough decision, especially when I'm facing a week's detention."

"Okay, okay," Principal Blanco grumbled. "I'll waive your detention."

"And I really think we should be able to call you Principal Shrinko," Barry added.

"Oh, all right." Principal Blanco sighed. "You can call me Principal Shrinko until Mr. Dirksen returns my head to its normal size. But after that I'm Blanco again. Is that a deal?"

"Deal." Barry and Principal Shrinko shook hands.

"Now, for the last time, what's your decision?" our principal asked.

"My decision is that we keep the lunch ladies," Barry said.

"Yay!" cheered the pro–lunch lady side.

"Boo!" groaned the pro–Vend-A-Lunch side.

"But I also think we should keep the Vend-A-Breakfast and Vend-A-Snack machines," Barry added.

Another wave of shocked silence swept over everyone left in the cafetorium.

"Is it my imagination, or did Barry Dunn propose a compromise?" Jessica asked.

Principal Shrinko took over the microphone

again. "Barry has proposed a compromise. I must say that I'm very impressed. Is there anything else you'd like to say, Barry?"

"Yeah. This is *still* what I think of school." Barry leaned toward the microphone and slid his hand into his armpit and made a disgusting noise.

"I should have known," Principal Shrinko groaned.

37

"I hear that Mr. Dirksen got the DITS/DUNCE working again," Josh said the next day. We were in the street in front of Andy's house. "He put a switch on it so he can use it as the DITS or the DUNCE."

"I guess that means we won't be able to call Blanco Shrinko much longer," I said as I strapped on my knee and elbow pads.

"Yeah, but you have to admit that it's been fun," Josh said as he pulled on his helmet.

"Hey, guys." Jessica and her friend Cathy came by. "What are you doing?"

"Andy still wants to see if the three of us can get on his BMX and ride backward," I said.

"Well, that's important," Jessica said and shared a wink with Cathy.

"So, are you happy with the compromise?" I asked my sister.

"The important question is, are *you* happy with it?" Jessica asked back.

"Sure," I said. "It seems like the best of both worlds."

Just then Andy came out of his driveway with his BMX. "What do you mean, *both* worlds? I thought there was only one world."

"It's just a figure of speech," I tried to explain.

"Since when does speech have a figure?" asked Josh.

"Hubba hubba." Andy grinned.

"Speech doesn't have a figure," I said. "Now, let's get this straight."

"Get *what* straight?" asked Josh.

"The track, dummy!" Andy cried.

"It doesn't have to be a straight track," I said. "It just has to be the *right* track."

"Why?" asked Josh. "What happened to the left track?"

Jessica and Cathy waved and went on their way. " 'Bye, guys."

I turned to my friends. "Listen, guys, you're way off base."

"Who is?" asked Andy.

"You are," I said.

"He's on base?" asked Josh.

"No, he's *off* base," I said.

"Which base?" asked Andy.

"Who's on first?" asked Josh.

"What's on second?" asked Andy.

"I give up," I groaned.

"Then I'll give down," said Andy.

"Okay, guys," I said wearily, "that's it."

"What's it?"

"*It's* it."

"It's *what*?"

"It."

"What?"

ABOUT THE AUTHOR

Todd Strasser has written many award-winning novels for young and teenage readers. Among his best-known books are *Help! I'm Trapped in Obedience School* and *Abe Lincoln for Class President*. His most recent books for Scholastic are *Help! I'm Trapped in a Movie Star's Body* and *Help! I'm Trapped in My Principal's Body*.

Todd speaks frequently at schools about the craft of writing and conducts writing workshops for young people. He and his family live outside New York City with their yellow Labrador retriever, Mac.

You can find out more about Todd and his books at http://www.toddstrasser.com